D1156801

Danny Dunn on a Desert Island

Also by Jay Williams and Raymond Abrashkin

DANNY DUNN AND THE
ANTI-GRAVITY PAINT

DANNY DUNN

on a

DESERT ISLAND

by Jay Williams & Raymond Abrashkin

Illustrated by Ezra Jack Keats

WHITTLESEY HOUSE

McGRAW-HILL BOOK COMPANY, INC.

NEW YORK   TORONTO   LONDON

This book is for Bobby and Wendy
with our affection

The authors wish to express their gratitude to Captain T. Scott Welton and Captain Theodore Winzer for advice and information on aeronautical matters. They are also indebted to William A. Burns and Paula Hutchison, whose work, *Man and His Tools*, provided a valuable reference in the writing of this book.

Library of Congress Catalog Card Number: 57-10924

Published by Whittlesey House
A division of the McGraw-Hill Book Company, Inc.
Printed in the United States of America

Contents

CHAPTER ONE

The Pie-Snatcher

It was a lovely afternoon during the first week of summer vacation. Birds warbled, a little breeze bent the heads of the dandelions, and on the window sill of Mrs. Dunn's kitchen a sweet-smelling huckleberry pie lay peacefully cooling in a tin plate. Then slowly and silently, from an upper window, a strange contraption began to descend upon the unsuspecting pie.

It was shaped like a cross of wood, slightly larger than the pie tin. From each of its four points a nail protruded, head down. Around each nail were many turns of fine insulated copper wire. Two copper wires led to batteries above. The whole thing was hung by a hook to a heavy cord.

The nails scraped the pie tin and suddenly froze to it like the powerful magnets they were. Above, there was the humming of a small motor from an Erector set, and slowly the pie began to rise, by a system of gears and pulleys, to the bedroom window over the kitchen.

Danny Dunn reeled in his prize. Carefully, he set it on the desk and ran his fingers through his red hair with a grin of triumph. He flipped a switch that turned off the power in his home-made electric crane, and removed the electro-magnets from the pie tin.

"Ha!" he said, rubbing his hands together. "I ought to patent this invention. Dunn's Special Super Pie-Snatching Apparatus."

He smacked his lips in anticipation. He opened the large blade of his scout knife and held it over the pie. But before he could cut himself a slice, a voice from the doorway broke in on him.

"Reach for the ceiling!" it said. "And if you drop that knife in my pie, you're a goner, podner."

Danny jumped guiltily and swung round. Then he said sadly, "Gee, Mom. How did you find out?"

"That," answered Mrs. Dunn firmly, taking up the pie, "is one of the trade secrets of being a mother."

"Are you going to take the *whole* thing away?" Danny wailed.

"I am."

"But I'm hungry."

"Nonsense!" said his mother. "You're just plain bored. That's what's turned you into a pie pirate. I'm not surprised, either. Sitting indoors on such a beautiful day!"

Mrs. Dunn shook her head. "Why don't you call Joe," she suggested, "and have a nice game of —well, of croquet?"

"I've played fifty games of croquet this week, and twenty-five games of ping-pong, and I went swimming and rode my bike and played baseball,

9

and now I haven't got anything to do," Danny blurted, scowling.

"That will soon change," said Mrs. Dunn, smiling. "You see, this is really a birthday pie."

"What do you mean? My birthday is past."

"I'll tell you a secret," his mother said. "Other people have birthdays, too. And tonight we're going to have a birthday party for Dr. Grimes."

"But Dr. Grimes is in Washington. Didn't Professor Bullfinch go there to visit him?"

"They're on their way back right now, together," said Mrs. Dunn. "The Professor called early this morning."

"Why didn't you tell me?" cried Danny.

"You were very busy working on an important scientific device," Mrs. Dunn twinkled.

"Not any more," said Danny. "The Professor's coming home! Yippee! Now there'll be some excitement around here."

Professor Euclid Bullfinch was Danny's hero. Ever since the boy could remember, he had wanted to become a scientist like the Professor. Mrs. Dunn, whose husband had died when Danny was a baby, was Professor Bullfinch's housekeeper. She ran the house on the edge of the campus of Midston University with a firm but gentle hand. And the Professor had been

10

Danny's first guide and teacher, and returned the boy's interest with pride and affection.

As for Dr. Grimes, he was an old friend of the Professor's, and a scientist, too. Like many close friends the two found great pleasure in arguing together over many issues.

"Well," said Mrs. Dunn, turning to the door, "I must get the guest room ready. Dr. Grimes is going to spend his vacation with us."

"Fine," Danny crowed. "I want to talk to him about my idea for a pocket electronic computer."

"You just stay out from under their feet," said Mrs. Dunn severely. "I'm sure they have important things to discuss. And I do hope they get here pretty soon."

"Are you worried, Mom?"

"Oh, not really. After all, the Professor has flown his plane a great many hours."

"It's Dr. Grimes's plane, too. They bought it together."

"I know. But I can imagine what arguments they have with those dual controls."

Mrs. Dunn broke off. There was a roar in the sky. Both she and Danny ran to the window. It overlooked a flat meadow near the house, on which a landing strip shone in the afternoon sun. On the far side of the meadow was a small hangar. As they stared from the window, a silvery airplane, a twin-motored, five-place Cessna, dropped toward the runway.

Suddenly it seemed to hesitate. Then, abruptly, it rose and banked to the left.

"It's the Professor and Dr. Grimes," Danny yelled. "And I'll bet they're arguing over the landing."

The plane shuddered, and just as suddenly banked to the right. Then it rose again, circled, and at last dropped to the runway with less than a foot to spare. It taxied a little way, swinging

first to one side and then the other, before coming to a stop.

"Thank goodness that's over," Mrs. Dunn

sighed. "Someday those two are going to argue themselves into real trouble."

But Danny wasn't listening. He was already halfway down the stairs, on his way to welcome the two scientists.

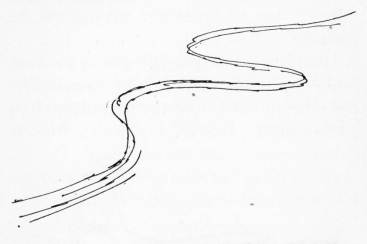

CHAPTER TWO

"I Challenge You . . ."

A few hours later, Professor Bullfinch and Dr. Grimes had stopped arguing, and for a very good reason—their mouths were full of huckleberry pie. Danny looked round at the familiar faces with a smile.

The Professor, bald and plump and jolly-looking, was patting his stomach, while his eyes twinkled merrily behind their black-rimmed glasses. Next to him sat Dr. Grimes, tall and bony, with a long, deeply wrinkled face which usually wore a sour expression but which tonight looked full of contentment. Joe Pearson, Danny's best friend, a thin boy with a rather sad face, was next to Danny; he was staring glassy-eyed at the remains of his third helping of pie. Mr. Pearson, Joe's father, a neat, blond man, was discussing rocket motors with Dr. Grimes, while Mrs. Pearson talked over recipes with redheaded Mrs. Dunn, Danny's mother.

Danny nudged his friend. "Now's the time, Joe," he whispered.

14

Joe got up slowly, pulling a sheet of paper from his pocket.

"Ladies and gentlemen," he said. "Can I have your attention?"

There was silence around the table.

"I'd like to read a poem I wrote," Joe went on. "It's a birthday poem for a good scientist and a fine friend. I guess it doesn't say everything it ought to—"

"Oh, Joe, stop worrying so much," Danny said. "Just read it."

Joe cleared his throat, and began:

"Even though he tries to look stern and
　　angry at all times,
Deep in his heart he is soft and sweet—
　　my pal, Dr. Grimes.
Just as a cowboy loves his horse and a criminal
　　loves his crimes,
That is how I feel about my pal,
　　Dr. A. J. Grimes.
For he is true blue—a friend through and
　　through,
And when it comes to science there is very little
　　he cannot do;
Oh, gold is where you find it, and silver
　　is found in dimes,

And I am very lucky to have found him,
   my pal, Dr. Grimes."

There was loud applause, and the Professor said, in mock horror, "Soft and sweet? You make him sound like a piece of fudge."

"Come, come, Bullfinch," Dr. Grimes said. "Don't run down my poem. After all, it isn't everyone who has a birthday poem written for him."

"Oh, well, it's just a little thing," Joe began.

"Not at all." Dr. Grimes spoke gruffly, but it was clear he was very pleased. "It was a splendid poem, Joe, and I'm grateful."

Mr. Pearson, who was an engineer, said with a chuckle, "You should have said, Joe, that when it comes to science there is very little he cannot do *theoretically*. After all, Dr. Grimes is a theoretician, not a practical scientist." Mr. Pearson considered himself to be extremely practical.

Dr. Grimes raised his eyebrows. "If you were talking about my friend Bullfinch," he said, "I could understand your point. But I, sir, am a most practical man."

Professor Bullfinch took his pipe out of his mouth. "The way you tried to land our plane

16

this afternoon almost made us both practical angels."

"Tut! You may be the nation's foremost authority on relativity, but I'm afraid you have an exaggerated notion of your flying ability, Bullfinch," Dr. Grimes retorted.

"Perhaps so—"

"You are nothing but a dreamer, as I've often told you."

"Oh, I'd hardly go that far," the Professor said quietly. "What about the hangar I built from a do-it-yourself kit?"

Danny and Joe looked at each other with smothered amusement. They remembered the Professor's struggles with the shedlike building.

Professor Bullfinch was unaware of their smiles. He leaned back in his chair, clasping his hands together. "It's not my aim to take over the functions of an engineer," he said, with an apologetic glance at Mr. Pearson. "However, I think a scientist ought to have a certain foundation in practical matters. If I were free to tell you why I went to Washington, you'd see that I am well on the way to applying theory to practice."

Dr. Grimes interrupted. "I have more than a foundation. As president of the Academy of

17

Scientific Research, I've made extensive studies in electricity, carpentry, plumbing, construction, mechanics, and half a dozen other fields. I dare say I could manage to make myself comfortable even on a—well, say, on a desert island. And with less to start with than Robinson Crusoe had."

"You couldn't use plumbing on a desert island," Mr. Pearson said thoughtfully. "Unless it was a desert island with a good hotel on it."

The Professor laughed. "My dear Grimes, I'm much too fond of you to want to see you perish on a desert island."

"Even one with a hotel on it?" asked Mr. Pearson.

"Even then. Whenever you decide to go," the Professor went on, "I'll go along with you, for I'm afraid you wouldn't last more than a day."

Dr. Grimes sat up straight. "Rubbish!" he exclaimed. "You go with me? Why, you're incapable of making your own bed."

"On a desert island," the Professor pointed out, "there'd be no need for making beds. Besides, that doesn't change the fact that in practical matters I have a little more experience—"

"Ha!" shouted Dr. Grimes. "Is that why you

18

wanted to land the plane practically on top of the hangar?"

"Tut, tut! Who actually landed it?"

"That's beside the point!" roared Dr. Grimes, pounding the table. "Why, on a desert island you'd starve to death."

"I don't think so," said the Professor, slowly. "Being practical only calls for a clear head and a calm mind—"

Dr. Grimes sprang to his feet in a rage. "Are you inferring that I ever lose my temper?" he shouted, red-faced. Then he stopped.

"This is too much," he said.

Deliberately, he threw down his napkin.

"Euclid Bullfinch," he said, in a grating voice, "I challenge you to a duel."

The others at the table, who had begun by smiling at the scientists' quarrel, now stared at Grimes in horror.

"What?" Professor Bullfinch fell back in his chair.

"A duel," repeated Dr. Grimes, "of desert islands!"

CHAPTER THREE

"Just Like Robinson Crusoe"

For a moment there was a stunned silence. Then Mr. Pearson, in his sharp, precise voice, said, "What would you do—throw them at each other?"

Dr. Grimes snorted. "Don't be absurd."

"But how—?" Mr. Pearson began.

"Very simple. I will go ashore on one desert island, and Bullfinch on another. After a time —say, a month—we'll see which of us has made himself more comfortable."

Danny and Joe stared at each other. "Oh, boy," whispered Danny, with shining eyes, "what an adventure!"

"Yeah," said Joe. "Ugh!"

Mrs. Dunn giggled. "I have an image in my mind of Mr. Bullfinch dressed in skins, like Robinson Crusoe, and with an umbrella made of leaves over his head. But I couldn't possibly send hot meals all the way to a desert island."

Professor Bullfinch looked meditatively into the bowl of his pipe. "I suppose," he said, "that you don't think I'd be capable of managing for myself? When I was younger I used to go on camping trips every summer."

"When you were younger, you used to have a full head of hair," sneered Dr. Grimes.

The Professor grinned, passing a hand over the few strands of hair that lay across his pink scalp. "Oh, that was an unkind cut, Grimes," he said. "I don't know . . . the idea sounds fairly attractive. I could do with a change of air, and a rest, and some solitude in which to think. Are you serious about this?"

"Never more serious in my life," said Dr. Grimes. "But you'd better put the idea of rest out of your mind. You'd be flying about like a split atom, just trying to keep alive."

"I don't think so. You might have a little trouble—"

Mr. Pearson shook his head. "In my opinion you'd both have trouble. It might be very dangerous."

"Why, Robinson Crusoe was shipwrecked," squeaked little Mrs. Pearson. "Would you have to start by being shipwrecked, too?"

"My reference to Robinson Crusoe a while ago," said Dr. Grimes, "was a figure of speech. Naturally, we wouldn't want this to be dangerous. For instance, we could arrange for someone

21

to check on us every day. And we'd have to take certain basic supplies."

"Yes," said the Professor, "we would have to start with enough equipment for our camps. Well, Grimes, if you really want to go through with this—"

"Are you trying to back out?"

"Not at all. We can each afford a month's vacation."

The Professor stood up and held out his hand. "I accept the challenge," he said.

"Oh, dear," cried Mrs. Pearson. "Are you going this minute?'

"Heavens! I hope not," said the Professor. "I was looking forward to a little music."

"We can settle the details tomorrow," Dr. Grimes agreed. "This is a birthday party, after all." He clapped the Professor on the shoulder. "It'll be a pleasure to beat you, my dear Bullfinch," he growled. "Just as it is a pleasure to play music with you."

The two were enthusiastic amateur musicians. They left the table and went into the living room where Professor Bullfinch got his big bull fiddle from a closet and tuned it, and Dr. Grimes took out his piccolo, fitted it together, and played a few practice trills. The ladies sat down on the couch to listen, and Mr. Pearson made himself

comfortable in an armchair and shut his eyes so that he could listen better.

The two scientists began to play a merry melody. Mr. Pearson listened so hard that soon his snores kept time to the music. Professor Bullfinch winked at Dr. Grimes, and they played a lullaby. Soon all disagreements were forgotten in the music.

Danny tugged Joe's sleeve and nodded toward the door. They slipped outside. The night was clear and starry, and a warm, moist breeze blew across the meadow, bringing with it a scent of sweet phlox, damp earth, and a hint of gasoline from the airplane hangar.

The boys climbed to the top of a tool shed in the garden. From here they could look over the dark bulk of the Professor's laboratory at the rear of the house, and see the spill of light from the front windows gilding the leaves of a lilac bush. The faint strains of the music came to them.

"Wouldn't it be great if they really did it?" said Danny. "Went to the desert island, I mean."

"I don't know," Joe said soberly. "It might be awfully lonely for them."

"Hm ... but maybe there would be savage cannibals, wild natives with spears, and we'd have to fight them off—"

"Huh?" Joe's head swiveled around. "How did *we* get on that desert island?"

"Not too hard, if we work it right. I could go with the Professor, and you can share Dr. Grimes's island."

"Gee, thanks. . . . Now wait a minute," cried Joe nervously. "Don't go jumping into things headfirst again. Every time you get that tone in your voice it means trouble. Like just last month, when you said, 'Maybe we can build a glider out of that orange crate and the toboggan.' Remember? Oh, golly, my back still hurts from the fall off this roof."

"Joe," said Danny gently, "you're a nice guy, but you have one fault. You worry too much."

"Well, but . . . savages, cannibals—"

"I was just joking."

"Oh, sure. But maybe they wouldn't be joking."

"Okay, Joe. I'll do it alone." And Danny slipped down from the roof. "I'm going in right now and ask my mother for permission to go along with the Professor."

Joe grinned. "You are?"

"Yes."

"Then forget about it. There isn't a chance in the world our folks would let us go."

"Don't be too sure," said Danny, as his friend joined him on the ground. "If we can talk them into it—"

"*We* again," Joe groaned. "Oh, all right. I guess I'll have to go along with you."

"Great! Just imagine"—and Danny struck a heroic pose—"Robinson Crusoe Dunn and Friday Pearson."

"Uh-huh. And Friday is supposed to be bad luck," Joe mumbled.

The two boys went back into the living room. The concert had just ended, and the Professor was lovingly polishing the body of his fiddle, as Dr. Grimes cleaned out his piccolo.

"Mom," said Danny, in a very sweet voice, "Joe and I were just thinking."

Mrs. Dunn raised one eyebrow. "One moment," she said. "A little bird tells me what it is. You both want to go along with the Professor and Dr. Grimes."

Danny's mouth dropped open. "Gosh!" he said.

"I think you'd better not, dear," said Mrs. Dunn.

"Absolutely not," said Mr. Pearson.

"Never!" Mrs. Pearson chimed in. "And that's final!"

CHAPTER FOUR

Plans and Preparations

"Gee, I'm glad our parents are letting us go on this trip," said Danny. He and Joe were sitting with Professor Bullfinch and Dr. Grimes at the dining-room table, a few days later.

"I'm not quite sure how you did it," said the Professor, lighting his pipe. "I would have wagered anything that Mr. and Mrs. Pearson, at least, would never have given in."

"That," said Danny, with a disarming grin, "is one of the trade secrets of being a kid."

"Yes, seems to me I can remember," chuckled the Professor. "Well, let's go over the arrangements so far. We must bear in mind that they only agreed to let you go if we could make the trip absolutely safe. Now, to begin with we'll fly our own plane to Lima, Peru. Off the coast some thirty or forty miles are the two islets we've called I.1 and I.2. As far as we know, they have no regular names. Both islands are uninhabited. We'll go out to them by boat. We will stay three weeks on the islands, Dr. Grimes and Joe on one, and Danny and I on the other. We'll be visited regularly by my friend Dr. Turbot, who will fly over from Lima. Furthermore, we'll be in radio communication with him every day, so no one need worry. Is that clear so far?"

"Quite clear," said Dr. Grimes. "And at the end of the three weeks, the winning pair will be chosen by Dr. Turbot and his associates. We'll be judged on the basis of how comfortable and secure we've made ourselves."

"Just so," the Professor nodded. "Now, let's make up a list of the equipment each team will take."

"I guess, if we want to be fair about it," said Danny, "each team ought to have the same equipment."

"Yes," agreed Professor Bullfinch. "I suppose we ought to make up categories and then fill in the details for each category."

He got out a large sheet of paper and at the top of it wrote, "Tools."

Joe, leaning across the table to see better, said, "That's the first category, eh?"

"Yes, I think it's the most important," said the Professor.

"What about weapons?" Dr. Grimes asked.

"Surely, defending ourselves against attack by savage beasts, or hunting—"

"But those *are* tools, my dear Grimes," the Professor replied mildly.

"Ah, yes. I see your point."

"Actually, we have only five categories that I can think of: tools, shelter, food, clothing, and first aid."

"How about something to do in our spare time?" Danny suggested.

"We may not have much spare time. However, perhaps we could take some books, games, schoolwork—"

"I wasn't exactly thinking of schoolwork," Danny replied.

"Let's discuss tools first," said Dr. Grimes. "I should think four rifles, four revolvers, bows and arrows—"

"Hold on!" the Professor interrupted. "We aren't an army, you know. There's probably nothing but small game on these islands. I should think a .22 rifle for each team would be ample."

"Suppose we meet cannibals, like Robinson Crusoe did?" Joe asked.

"That's unlikely," said Dr. Grimes. "The islands are uninhabited." He turned to Professor Bullfinch. "For the time being, I agree. What else?"

"We ought to choose only the most basic tools." The Professor drew thoughtfully at his pipe, and puffed out a great cloud of blue smoke. "If we're to do this right, we must take along simple and necessary things, enough to make ourselves comfortable, but not enough to burden ourselves down. For example, a crowbar—"

"What? But that's a house-wrecking tool," said Joe. "Are we going to wreck our houses before we even build them?"

"Let me finish, Joe," Professor Bullfinch said amiably. "I was about to say that a crowbar is an example of a good, basic tool. It's true, it can be used as a wrecking bar. It can also be used as a lever, a hole digger, a ground breaker, a kind of club or spear, a tent pole, or even an anchor."

"Then you think we ought to take a crowbar?" asked Dr. Grimes.

"No, I don't."

"But you just said—"

"Actually, any strong wooden pole would do just as well," said the Professor. "I was just pointing out the kind of tool we want, a tool with many uses. You see, we'll be starting where, say, the pioneers started. They opened up the wilderness with just a few tools, and made everything else they needed."

"They always had an ax," said Danny.

"Yes. I think we need axes and good stout knives."

"We ought to have a couple of those folding shovels," said Joe. "After all, we don't want to have to dig with our hands."

"Good," the Professor said, writing all these things down.

"Another sort of tool would be short-wave radios," said Dr. Grimes. "We'll need them to keep in touch with the mainland."

The Professor nodded. "Tools to cook with —pots, pans, forks, and spoons."

"Messkits," said Danny. "And flashlights."

"Saws, hammers, and nails," Joe added.

"And plenty of cord and rope," Danny finished.

They all sat in thought for a moment, and then the Professor said, "That seems like enough. Now we come to shelter. Tents?"

"Don't forget ground-cloths and blankets," said Danny.

"For food we can take dehydrated stuff," said Dr. Grimes. "And army-type K rations and canned rations."

"Yes, and we should take some vitamin pills along as a supplement," said the Professor.

"We ought to have towels, extra shoes, raincoats, and hats," said Dr. Grimes.

"And plenty of bandages, antiseptics, and a snakebite kit," Danny put in, remembering his Boy Scout training.

"Phew!" The Professor exclaimed. "I've got writer's cramp. Wait a minute and let me rest."

He put down his pencil and massaged his hand. "I'm sure this list will grow before we're ready to leave," he said. "When I began by saying we should take only simple and necessary things, I didn't quite realize how much is necessary."

"It's too bad, in a way," Danny mused, "that we can't just junk it all and start from scratch, with nothing."

The Professor leaned back in his chair, with a laugh. "My boy," he said, "Dr. Grimes and I are having a duel to see which of us is more practical. For heaven's sake, let's not consider it a duel to the death."

He fumbled in an inner pocket and brought

out a small calendar. "Now, then," he said. "Let's give ourselves a week in which to get these things together and make all our preparations."

"A week?" Joe repeated. "Then I'd better get busy."

"You mean, getting your things together?"

"No, eating. I want to have plenty to fall back on."

"Gee, Joe," Danny said, shaking his head. "How can you be so crazy about food and stay so thin?"

"It's because I worry so much about what's for dinner," Joe explained.

"Very well," said the Professor, getting to his feet. "One week to prepare. In one week, the duel will commence."

CHAPTER FIVE

The Duel Begins

On a bright clear day, one week later, the four travelers gathered at the hangar near Professor Bullfinch's house. With them were Mrs. Dunn, the Pearsons, and several other friends who had come to see them off. A great heap of equipment lay ready to be stowed away in the plane.

Professor Bullfinch, in khaki shorts and shirt, tapped out his pipe on the heel of his boot. He seemed as calm as if a trip to a desert island were an everyday occurrence.

"The time has come to say our good-byes," he said. "Remember, we'll be in radio communication with Dr. Turbot, in Lima, every day so you parents needn't worry. Are there any last-minute questions?"

"Yes," said Mrs. Pearson, dabbing at her eyes with a handkerchief. "Can't you change your minds and stay home?"

"Oh, Ma," Joe protested. "Don't start that again."

"They'll be perfectly safe, Sarah," said Mr. Pearson, patting her hand.

"I know it. But saying good-bye always makes me feel so sad."

"If there are no other questions," said the Professor, "we'd better get everything aboard."

They turned to the mountain of equipment. In addition to the material they needed for their camps, there were numerous cans of gasoline, and a rubber raft with a box of emergency equipment.

They got the gasoline aboard first, and then the Professor put his hand on a large packing case. "I'm afraid this won't go through the door," he said. "What on earth is it, anyway?"

"The two portable cookstoves we decided on," said Dr. Grimes.

"Hm. This plane carries a little over a thousand pounds. With three hundred pounds of gasoline, for emergencies, we're dangerously close to the load limit."

Danny said, "Why not just leave them behind, Professor? We can build a fireplace."

"I only agreed to them for your sake," growled Dr. Grimes. "I can do without them very well."

"That suits me," said the Professor. "Let's move them aside."

"As far as that goes," Dr. Grimes continued, "we don't need air mattresses, or pillows, either."

"I agree," the Professor said. "And since the islands are near the equator and will be quite warm, we can do without tents. After all, the most important part of adapting to a desert island should be making one's own shelter."

"Leave them behind then," cried Dr. Grimes. "It will only make it easier for me to win."

"Here! Wait a second," Mr. Pearson said. He stepped between the two scientists and held up his hands. "If you two practical men go on this way you'll find yourselves on those islands with nothing but loincloths and hunting knives, like a character in a TV jungle story. We don't care so much about your comfort, but I'm sure Mrs. Dunn feels as my wife and I do—we want our boys to survive."

That put an end to the competition, and they packed the rest of the gear away in the plane. At last they were ready to depart. Joe hugged his mother and father. Danny gave his mother a last embrace, and whispered, "Don't worry, Mom. We'll be all right. It'll just be a swell vacation."

"I'm not really worried," said Mrs. Dunn, with a wistful smile. "After all, you've gone camping almost every summer. Just be careful. Do try not to get wet or chilled. And—look after Mr.

Bullfinch, dear. He is a very important scientist, but he doesn't have quite as much experience in camping as you do."

Danny was flattered. "I will," he promised earnestly.

He gave his mother a last kiss, and followed Joe into the plane. The scientists, after shaking hands all around, took their seats at the controls. The twin motors roared, and the plane slowly taxied down the runway.

Since the Cessna was only a small plane, as private planes go, the two scientists had decided to make the trip over land as much as possible. They flew to Brownsville, Texas; then over Mexico and Central America, keeping to a schedule of between five and six flying hours a day. At night, too tired for sightseeing, they slept in hotels near the airfields where they landed for refueling and checkups. The evening of the fifth day found them within a hundred miles of their goal.

They were flying down the west coast of South America, with the towering ranges of the Andes Mountains on their left and the Pacific Ocean on their right, when the first heavy drops of rain slashed across the windshield. Professor Bullfinch, who was at the controls, tried to get above the clouds.

The wind increased, until the plane was rocking and bumping madly. The rain on the plastic canopy above them made a continuous beating noise that almost drowned out speech.

"See if you can raise Lima on the radio," the Professor shouted.

Dr. Grimes shook his head. He had been working over the radio, trying to contact the field, but from the machine came nothing but crackles and squeals. "Something's wrong with it," he said.

Danny peered over the Professor's shoulder. "Weren't we flying due south?" he cried. "Because I think we're going due west now."

"Difficult to tell from the compass alone," the Professor replied. "I'm afraid we're being blown out to sea, though. If we could only get the control tower at the field."

"Better reduce power," said Dr. Grimes. "This high wind puts a lot of stress on the wings."

Suddenly the engine began to sputter and backfire. The Professor leaned forward to look at the instrument panel. "We're losing altitude," he said. "It must be the cylinder heads. The rain has cooled them down."

"Put the mixture controls in 'Full Rich,' " Dr. Grimes cried.

"Can you see anything below?"

It was pitch-dark by now, and in any case the rain would have made visibility difficult.

"I think we're over the sea," said the Professor. "We'll have to gain some altitude." He pulled back on his wheel.

"Nonsense!" Dr. Grimes barked. "We've got to land."

He shoved forward on his controls. He was a little stronger than the Professor. The plane quivered like a live thing and headed downward. The boys were thrown forward against the backs of the pilots' seats.

"Let go!" the Professor said.

"You let go!" Dr. Grimes was equally insistent.

The nose of the plane dipped suddenly. The Professor, dragging back on the controls, managed to level it out at the last moment.

There was a splash that sent water thundering over the canopy.

"We've fallen into the sea!" Danny shouted into the stunned silence.

The lights on the instrument panel flickered and died. The Professor seized a flashlight.

"Get the life raft out, quickly," he commanded. "We don't know how much time we have before the plane sinks."

Danny and Joe got the folded raft from its rack. Meantime, Dr. Grimes was struggling with the door on his side.

"Seems to be jammed," he grunted.

Water was already seeping over the floor. The Professor lent his weight, and he and Dr. Grimes forced the door open. Danny passed the raft bundle to Dr. Grimes, who first fastened its rope to the plane and then pressed the trigger. Then he threw it out into the sea. By the beam of the Professor's flashlight they could see it bobbing in the water. Rain dashed into their faces.

Joe yelled, "What about the supplies?"

"Don't try to get them all," said the Professor. "Just grab whatever you can and let's go. We're sinking."

While the men held the raft close to the cockpit by its rope, the two boys stepped down into it. Dr. Grimes passed them some boxes and bundles, and then he and the Professor stepped across into the raft. They pulled in the rope.

Just in time. The tail of the plane tilted high, and then the whole craft slid down into the sea.

CHAPTER SIX

The Island

The first rays of the sun danced across the waves, making the sea sparkle like an emerald, and turning the little rubber raft into a golden boat. The four voyagers, damp and chilled and weary, lifted their faces to the warmth of the new day and felt life return to their limbs.

Professor Bullfinch looked slowly about the horizon. "Not a sign of land," he said. "But then, I didn't expect to see any. We have drifted during the night."

"Thank heaven the rain stopped," Dr. Grimes said. "I thought for a while we were going to be filled and sunk."

"I wonder where we are?" said Danny, shifting his position cautiously. It was a strange sensation to know that nothing but a thin skin of rubberized canvas separated him from the Pacific Ocean. He took out his compass. "South is that way."

"What good does that do us?" Dr. Grimes said glumly. "We don't know how far off course we

41

were blown, or in what direction. We don't know which way we drifted, nor how far."

"Still, we're lucky," said Professor Bullfinch, with his customary tranquillity. "We were able to launch the raft. Fortunately, the plane fell in the sea. . . ."

"Fortunately?" Joe said. "What's so fortunate about it?"

"Mountain peaks are a good deal harder to fall on," the Professor said drily.

"Oh. That's right."

"We were lucky, too, that we were able to put a few things into the raft," the Professor went on. "For instance, that box of army K rations. Why not open it now, Joe, and let's all have breakfast."

Joe didn't need to be invited twice. He cut open the waterproof wrapping of the box with his pocketknife, and passed out the flat containers. Each held a bar of dried meat, a bar of chocolate, and a bar of dried fruit, as well as some jam, crackers, and either lemonade powder or powdered coffee.

As they munched, some large brown birds appeared, balancing in the air above the raft, their long wings moving silently as they kept themselves aloft.

"Vultures!" Joe cried, with his mouth full. "Go away! We're not dead yet."

"They aren't vultures," said the Professor, "but boobies."

"How do you know they're boobies? They haven't done anything stupid yet."

"It's only what they're called, Joe."

"They certainly look beautiful in flight," said Danny. "Look how their wings catch the air currents."

"They'd look more beautiful in a plate with gravy and mashed potatoes," Joe grinned.

"I don't think you'd enjoy them. They are fish-eaters, and they have a strong, fishy taste," said the Professor.

"We couldn't cook them in the raft anyway," Danny added.

"Gee, that's right," said Joe. "We haven't any potatoes."

Danny sat erect so suddenly that the raft trembled. "Birds!" he exclaimed. "Of course!"

"Take it easy, Dan. You'll upset us," the Professor cautioned.

"But Professor, listen! If there are birds, maybe we're near shore. After all, they have to nest somewhere."

"Why, it's true that boobies nest on shore," the Professor said. "But I don't know—"

"It doesn't matter," Joe put in gloomily. "There's another storm coming, and we'll probably be swamped this time."

"A storm?"

"Sure. Look at that big cloud over there."

The Professor stared. Then he exclaimed, "That's the land!"

"Ooh, he's gone crazy," Joe moaned. "He can't tell solid land from a cloud. Next he'll be seeing camels and palm trees!"

"Not at all," the Professor said, shaking his head. "You will observe that that cloud isn't moving. It's the warm air rising from the ground and condensing in the upper atmosphere."

"You're right!" Dr. Grimes said. "It must be at least two and a half or three miles away, since that's as far as one can see over the earth's curve from a height like ours. Let's make for it. We may have a long way to paddle."

There were paddles stowed in the bottom of the raft, and each of them seized one. They had to reach out over the inflated sides of the raft to touch the water, so that paddling was an awkward job. Joe and Danny took the front, and the Professor and Dr. Grimes, with their longer arms

44

and stronger strokes, the rear. It took them a little while to get the rhythm and dip their paddles in unison. Danny called out the stroke like a coxswain.

After an hour they could see the loom of the land. Another hour of hot, continuous labor brought them close enough to make out that it was a large island towering up to a peak in the center. They could see the white foam of breakers at the foot of cliffs, and they began paddling their little craft along the coastline while still some distance away.

"There. That looks like a beach where we can land," Joe said.

They all saw the white gleam of sand among the reddish-brown rocks. They were dripping with sweat, but the harder they paddled, the slower they seemed to go. The tide was against them. They struggled on, until they drew near the arms of a bay that sheltered the little beach.

"When we get into that cove, the waves will carry us the rest of the way," Dr. Grimes panted.

"If they don't dash us against the rocks," cautioned the Professor. "Be ready to steer—"

A point of jagged stone stuck up out of the water a few yards ahead. Even as he spoke, the crest of a great comber rushed them straight for it.

"That's the land."

For an instant it seemed they would be hurled upon it. Both Danny and Joe thrust out their paddles. The raft almost capsized; there was a jarring thump, but the paddles held firm and they heaved themselves past the rock.

The next wave carried them almost to the beach. The boys scrambled overboard into the surf, and pulled the raft up on the sand.

"Whew! Solid ground!" said Danny.

Joe knelt down and kissed the beach. "I always hated sand in my mouth before," he said, "but now—I love you, island."

The Professor, shading his eyes with his hand, was peering about. The other three, falling silent, turned to look, too.

They stood on a small crescent-shaped beach, no more than fifty paces long and perhaps ten wide. On either side of them two arms of jumbled reddish blocks of stone stretched down to the water. Beyond were steep cliffs, rising fifteen or twenty feet straight out of the water to ledges where a few plants had seized a foothold. Inland, where the beach ended, thorny trees and cactus grew among the rocks, and farther on, a regular jungle of dark, dense trees began. The ground sloped sharply upward and in the distance, among masses of foliage, a single mountain peak rose, bare and menacing.

From the jungle came the whistles and calls of unfamiliar birds, and nearer at hand, among the rocks, great lizards with spiky crests scuttled away. A huge turtle, large enough for Danny to sit on, lumbered swiftly down to the sea, plunged in like a barge, and disappeared.

In the face of that peaceful but utterly strange scene, the four travelers drew closer together.

"Wonder where we are?" Joe said at last.

"At a guess," said Dr. Grimes, "I would say we were somewhere in or near the Galapagos Islands."

"You're probably right," the Professor agreed. "If our plane was blown westward, and our raft was carried still farther westward on the current, the Galapagos Islands would be the likeliest land. They are chiefly volcanic islands, and this appears to be so. Furthermore, those lizards—iguanas, I believe—and those thorny trees are quite typical of the Galapagos Islands."

"Then we are on, or near, the equator," Dr. Grimes said.

"Yes. Anywhere from six to eight hundred miles from the mainland. That is, if this is really one of the Galapagos."

They picked up the precious raft and carried it well up out of reach of the tide. Then they unloaded it, setting their supplies out in a neat row.

49

Danny said, "I think we ought to explore. Let's find out how big the island is."

"No," Joe grumbled. "Not until we've got some meals planned."

"Ridiculous!" Dr. Grimes exploded. "We don't know where we are. There may be savage beasts, or even savage people. Security is our most important concern. Every stranger must be considered an enemy—"

"I don't agree," said the Professor. "I'll consider my surroundings friendly until they're proved otherwise."

"But we must have weapons," Dr. Grimes insisted. "Our rifles are gone with the plane. We ought to make spears, bows, or clubs—"

"If there are strangers, our weapons will only bring out their weapons," the Professor said. "I think a shelter would be the best idea. I don't like the idea of sleeping out in the open. What if there's a storm?"

"But a shelter's no good unless we have something to eat in it," Joe complained.

"What about fresh water?" Danny put in.

"Spears and bows—" Dr. Grimes repeated.

"We need a fire, too."

"That's right, but we ought to have something to cook over it—" said Joe.

"A fire—"

"Spears—"

"Food—"

"*Quiet!*" snapped the Professor, in so loud and sharp a tone that the others jumped. They had rarely heard him raise his voice.

He glanced from one to another. Then he smiled. "I'm sorry," he said. "I didn't mean to sound angry, but I had no choice. It appears that the very first thing we need is government."

"Government? Are you out of your mind?" said Dr. Grimes.

"I don't think so. Are we going to be a democracy or a—a kingdom? Because if we are a democracy, then we ought to decide all important issues—such as what we ought to do and when to do it—by voting. That way we'll save time and do what most of us think ought to be done."

"Okay with me," said Danny, and Joe nodded.

Dr. Grimes frowned. "Do you think the boys should have equal votes with us?"

"Why not? They'll have to work just as hard as we will."

"Hm! Very well. I agree. Let's put the matter to a vote."

"Before we do that," said the Professor, "I suggest that we make a list. Let's see. The inside of this K-ration carton will do."

He ripped out a square of waxed cardboard,

51

then he took a stub of pencil from his pocket.

"Food, water, shelter, weapons," he said as he wrote. "Hm! Seems to me I made this list once before! Anything else?"

"Exploring," said Danny.

"We'll do that as we search for food and water, I should think. What else?"

"Building a signal fire," said Dr. Grimes.

"Yes. Anything more? Then let's begin."

When the votes were taken, it was found that all four of them agreed that fresh water and a shelter came first. They still had some K rations left, so food could be postponed for the time being. As for weapons, and signaling, all but Dr. Grimes voted to put them off for the moment.

"That's settled, then," said the Professor. "I'll put the list in this box, and if anything more occurs to us we can jot it down and vote on it later. Now, since water and a shelter come first, I suggest that we divide into two parties. Suppose Dan and I tackle the shelter. And Grimes, there's a collapsible bucket in the raft; why don't you and Joe search for fresh water?"

Dr. Grimes nodded.

"One more thing," said the Professor earnestly. "Whatever you do—be careful. We don't know what lies in that jungle."

CHAPTER SEVEN

Back to the Stone Age

When Joe and Dr. Grimes had gone, the Professor and Danny climbed up to a ledge on the fringe of the forest. Here there was a kind of pocket of earth where some coarse grass grew, and from this point they could look down upon the beach and over the tumbled expanse of smooth rocks.

"Most of that is lava flow," the Professor explained. "This island obviously is an extinct volcano."

"Well, I hope it doesn't decide to go back in business," said Danny. Then, more seriously, he added, "Oh, I wanted to ask you something, Professor Bullfinch."

"What is it, Dan?"

"Well, is the duel between you and Dr. Grimes still on?"

Professor Bullfinch glanced at him in surprise. "The duel? Why, I'd forgotten all about it."

"I know we're all on the same island, but—"

"It isn't a game any more, Danny," the Pro-

53

fessor said soberly, putting his hand on the boy's shoulder.

"I know that."

"It may be very serious indeed." He gave a little snort. "I am just remembering all the things we thought were basic and necessary when we were planning the trip. Now we're without anything."

"Then you mean we'd better forget about the duel?" Danny asked, a little sadly.

Professor Bullfinch said, "Hmm. I didn't say that. It might make our wits sharper, you know. Give us something to aim for, each day. Keep us on our toes, as you might say. I think perhaps— well, I think perhaps we ought to do it, provided Dr. Grimes is willing, of course."

Danny brightened. "Swell! That's great. Now let's make a shelter that'll show how good you are."

The Professor surveyed the ledge. It was protected on one side by a ridge, or hump, of boulders, and at its back rose the tree-covered hill.

"I thought," he said, "of a modest little place. Four bedrooms, perhaps, and a sort of common room which could be made into a laboratory—"

Danny raised his eyebrows. "That would take a lot of lumber. And I'm not sure we could get it done by tonight. . . ."

"Er—no, perhaps not. A single room, then, with four bunk-beds."

"We can't make beds, Professor. We'd need a saw and a plane, and bedsprings, and mattresses. And even putting up four walls and a roof would be a lot of work."

The Professor scratched his nose thoughtfully. "I may be a bit too ambitious," he admitted, with a sigh. "I am thinking too far ahead. I suppose a simple lean-to would be best."

"There are some thin, tall young trees growing up on the hill," Danny said. "But even that will be hard to do without an ax."

Professor Bullfinch sat down on a rock, and absently put his empty pipe between his teeth. "Wish I'd thought to fill my pockets with tobacco," he said. "Look here, Dan. Do you remember our talk about tools before we started this trip?"

"Yes, I do."

"It strikes me that we're back at the beginnings of mankind. Robinson Crusoe had the tools he'd saved from the wreck, but we have almost nothing. A couple of pocketknives, some rope, and some fishhooks. We're almost where Stone Age men started. And we have the same equipment they had."

"What equipment did Stone Age men have?"

"Their hands, my boy. And stone and wood. You see, most animals can live in only one kind of environment. Monkeys live in trees and are good climbers; moles live in the ground and have built-in shovels for digging. But men can live anywhere at all, because they have hands and memories and imaginations. So they can invent tools to help them adapt to any sort of surroundings. We can survive here by inventing tools."

Danny nodded slowly. "Invent a house-building tool?"

"Of course. An ax is a sort of house-building tool."

"But we haven't any steel, or any way to forge it."

"I know, Danny. But I said before that we are back in the Stone Age. Now these islands are volcanic, so perhaps we can find some obsidian."

"Obsidian? Oh, yes, the Indians made arrowheads out of it. It's volcanic glass, isn't it?"

"Exactly. It's very hard, and forms a sharp edge when broken. Perhaps we can make a stone ax."

"Have you ever made one?" Danny asked.

"Er—no. But I know the theory. Let's try it."

They searched about among the spiky plants

until at last Danny found a chunk of dark-brown, glassy-looking stone as large as a football. A piece was broken off one end, and the inside was almost as shiny as a mirror.

Without thinking, Danny dashed it against a large black rock that rose out of the earth. The obsidian flew apart with a crack and splinters of it sailed past the Professor's legs.

"Oh, gosh! I'm sorry," Danny gulped. "I guess I wasn't thinking."

"I'm afraid not," the Professor said, looking ruefully at the many small bits of stone. "Remember, Dan, a scientist must not jump head-long into something. Luckily, none of them hit me."

He bent over. "Ah, you were doubly lucky. Here's one piece that might do, with a little shaping."

He had found a lump somewhat larger than his hand, thick at one end with a sharp, brittle razor edge at the other. He got a piece of lava and slowly chipped away bits of obsidian until he had made a rough, wedge-shaped head. Meantime, Danny went a little way into the forest and broke off a tough branch about three feet long. With his pocketknife he trimmed off the twigs and split one end of it, carving away some of the

57

wood on the inside of the cleft so that the axhead could be wedged into it without splitting the wood all the way down.

"Now," said the Professor, "let's see if it works."

He forced the stone head into the cleft and tied it firmly in place, using some of the light, strong line from the raft's emergency chest.

He bowed to Danny. "Will you try first, or shall I?" he asked with a smile.

"After you, Professor," Danny answered.

The Professor swung the ax, and brought it down at an angle in the trunk of a sapling. It bit deep.

He let go the handle. "My goodness!" he exclaimed in astonishment. "It works!"

"Didn't you know it would?" Danny said.

The Professor cleared his throat. "Theory and practice don't always go hand in hand," he said. "I wasn't sure."

Their talk ended abruptly as two figures came into view between the trees. Danny shaded his eyes and stared.

"It's Dr. Grimes," he said. "And he has some kind of strange animal with him—like a big, piebald monkey!"

CHAPTER EIGHT

Home, Sweet Home

It wasn't strange that Danny didn't recognize his friend. Joe's face and arms were covered with a film of green-brown mud. He wore no shirt, and the white color of his chest was startling against the dark mud. He carried what looked like a dirty old burlap bag, but when he came closer they could see it was his shirt, full of large, melon-shaped fruits.

"What on earth—" the Professor began.

"We found a stream," Joe interrupted. "And these fruits. There are lots more back up in the woods. Bananas, too, growing right on the trees."

"If you found a stream," the Professor remarked, "why didn't you wash yourself off?"

Joe looked down at himself. "I tried," he said ruefully. "The stuff's sticky, like glue. It won't come off."

"What happened?" asked Professor Bullfinch.

"We climbed up the rocks until we entered the forest," Dr. Grimes explained. "It's hard going; most of the plants are mimosa, or cactus, or simi-

59

lar thorny shrubs and trees. But up above there's a kind of rain forest. It's much warmer there, and there's grass and some flowers."

"And you ought to see the birds," Joe put in. "All kinds, and they're almost tame. They flew right down to us."

Dr. Grimes nodded. "I am certain there are no other people on this island. The birds have never seen men before. We found a little river and a number of groves of papaya and banana, as well as some other fruits I believe to be a species of mango. Joe climbed one of the papaya trees. They have a smooth trunk and no lower branches, and he lost his footing and fell. It's quite swampy there, and he landed on his front in the mud."

"Then we followed the stream down," Joe said. "It comes out on the other side of those rocks and falls to a shelf about twenty feet below, and then into the sea. You can't see it from here because of that ridge of rock."

Dr. Grimes had brought back a bucket full of water. He hung it in the shade and looked about him. "This is a good spot for a camp," he said. "But where's the shelter you were going to build? I'm afraid, my dear Bullfinch, you were not as practical as we."

60

"On the contrary, we've already made the first tool," said the Professor complacently, and pointed to the stone ax, still embedded in the tree trunk.

All four now went to work in earnest on the shelter. Using the ax, the Professor cut two long, slender saplings, trimming away the branches to leave a fork at the top of each. With their pocketknives the boys sharpened the bottoms. Then Danny tried to push one of them into the ground.

"You ought to have made a stone hammer," Joe said, as Danny puffed over the work. "Let's find a hunk of stone and make a pounding tool."

Professor Bullfinch, wiping his streaming forehead, was standing nearby. He smiled, and held up the ax. "What do you think this is?" he said.

"Why, you said it was an ax."

The Professor turned it in his hand. "One edge is sharp, yes, but the back is blunt. Isn't it a hammer as well?"

Danny whistled. "Oh, what a dope I am!" he said.

"Not at all. You simply judge by the look of a thing, and by what people say of it. As a scientist you should keep an open mind."

Using the back of the ax, they drove the uprights into the ground and laid another long pole

61

across the forks. Then they cut a number of other branches and tied them along the top pole slantwise, with their ends resting on the ground.

They stood back to examine their work with pride.

"It's not pretty," Joe remarked, "but it's home. I wonder for how long?"

"Not long, let us hope," said the Professor. "Our original plan was excellent, but I hardly expected to be marooned."

Dr. Grimes said, "I think we ought to take stock of our supplies and see what we have. We may have to stay here for several weeks."

They all went down to the beach, where they had left the raft and their supplies. They had saved pitifully little. There was a single blanket, and a cardboard box in which twenty K-ration cartons remained. There was the raft's emergency chest, containing fishhooks, signal flares, a repair kit containing glue and patches, the folding bucket, a large first-aid kit, a flashlight, a compass, and fifty feet of light strong cord. There were two empty canteens, a coil of nylon rope, and a large knife with a cork handle.

There was also a waterproof sack containing something that looked like a ukelele with the

All four went to work in earnest

neck broken off. Dr. Grimes pounced on this with an exclamation of pleasure.

"This may prove the best tool of all," he said. "It's the emergency radio transmitter. Now we'll be able to signal our location."

"Excellent," said Professor Bullfinch. "Now then, let's all empty our pockets. Almost everything we own may turn out to be useful."

He himself was the first to do so. He had a handkerchief, many scraps of paper and old envelopes covered with scribbled notes and formulae, a small slide rule, a pocket watch—ruined by the salt water—some loose change, a few pencils, a fountain pen with no ink in it, a wallet, the stub of a ticket to a lecture, and some keys.

"We could use these," Danny said, picking up one of the keys, "for arrowheads, if we sharpened them."

Dr. Grimes was next. The contents of his pockets were much the same as those of the Professor, except for dozens of membership cards to various scientific organizations, and a small volume entitled *The Home Gardener's Handy Handbook*.

Joe's pockets contained some Life Savers, a pocketknife, a single peanut, a couple of bottle caps, the top of a cereal box with a contest jingle on it which Joe had forgotten to mail before they left home ("Ooh, there goes my chance for a Geiger counter," he grumbled when he found it), some string, a Second-Class Scout badge with the pin broken off, and several erasers.

"Why so many erasers, Joe?" the Professor asked gently.

Joe shrugged. "Because I'm a pessimist, I guess."

Danny's pockets, however, made up for everything. He had some wire and some strong cord, a few nails, several foreign coins, an airmail stamp, a magnifying glass, a few watch gears, some nuts and bolts, two pieces of very dry chewing gum, and best of all, a small emergency kit in which were a needle and thread, some gauze and adhesive tape, and a dozen waterproof matches.

"This is a regular treasure trove," said the Professor cheerfully. "Every expedition should have a Danny with it."

They carried everything up what was rapidly becoming a cleared trail, to their camp on the ledge. They stored the food and emergency chest away in the rear of the lean-to. They spread out the blanket as a ground sheet. A little distance away they built a fireplace of stones. It began to look quite cosy and home-like when they had finished.

"Why don't you boys go fill your canteens so we'll have extra water?" the Professor suggested. "Then we can have some lunch and set up the transmitter."

"What's for lunch?" Joe asked.

"The papayas you brought back, and K rations."

"That's what I was afraid of. Maybe Danny and I ought to go fishing this afternoon."

"Not a bad idea. And by the way, Joe, try to wash some more of that mud off yourself. As a scientist I'm used to peculiar smells, but. . . ."

"It'll wear off after a while," Joe said carelessly.

"Mmhm. I suppose it will."

The two boys went off, and the Professor opened the raft chest and took out the work list they had made.

"There is one more thing I want to put on this list," he remarked to Dr. Grimes. And in large letters he wrote: SOAP.

CHAPTER NINE

Adventure at Sea

When lunch was over, Dr. Grimes got the water-proof bag and took out the emergency transmitter. It was about a foot high, with a folding crank on the top of it. In front were some switches and a small, round door which Dr. Grimes opened; inside was a reel of aerial wire.

"This radio," he said, examining the instruction booklet, "puts out a signal on the international distress frequency of five hundred kilocycles. All ships keep a constant watch—or rather, listen—on that frequency, so that sooner or later one is bound to hear us. To begin with, we must put up the antenna."

A balloon for raising the antenna was included in the kit, and when they had inflated it with the hydrogen-making device that came in the bag, they attached the antenna wire to it and let it go aloft. Dr. Grimes then sat down on the emergency chest, which was made of plywood. He put the transmitter between his thighs and strapped it into place to hold it steady. He set the switch at position One, which sent out an automatic SOS, and began turning the crank.

"Faster," said the Professor. "The instructions say that this light will go on when you have reached a sufficient speed to work the generator."

Dr. Grimes cranked grimly, his lean face red with exertion. All at once, a light flashed on at the front of the set. The Professor bent over and adjusted a knob. The light grew brighter.

"Good. Now we're transmitting at maximum frequency," said the Professor.

"I can keep this up for another twenty minutes or so," Dr. Grimes said, "and then someone else will have to take over."

"We'll all take turns at it," the Professor replied. "Fifteen minutes each, three times a day, will give us three hours of broadcast. . . . Where are you going, Joe?"

Joe, who had been edging away, mumbled, "I thought Danny and I were going fishing. Dinner, you know. . . ."

"You can go after your fifteen minutes are over," said the Professor firmly.

About an hour later, the two boys dragged the raft down to the water's edge and climbed aboard. They had fishhooks and lines fastened to light poles, and for bait they had mussels which they had found growing among the rocks in the sea.

As they paddled away from shore Joe said mournfully, "If we have to keep up that signaling every day I won't care whether I'm rescued or not. Even my blisters have blisters."

"I've been thinking about that," Danny said.

"What, my blisters? Gee, thanks a lot."

"Not your blisters. That transmitter. Listen, Joe, this is better than the original plan of two islands, isn't it?"

"I have a feeling there's trouble coming," Joe groaned.

"It's not trouble. Wouldn't you like to stay here a while?"

"It depends. If we can get something besides K rations to eat, for instance—"

"All right. You remember what Professor Bullfinch said about the ax? That we shouldn't judge a tool by its appearance?"

"So?"

"So maybe that radio transmitter can be used in a different way."

"You mean to receive broadcasts? Like baseball games—"

"No, no. I mean, instead of using it as a tool to get us off the island, maybe it can be used to keep us here."

"I don't get it," Joe said.

"If something went wrong with it," said Danny, "we couldn't send our position. Then we'd have to stay on this island. Wouldn't we?"

"But what could go wrong?"

"Well, if the crank were to disappear, for instance. . . ."

"Why should it disappear?"

"Oh, for heaven's sake, Joe," said Danny. "Because I'd take it off and hide it in the sand."

Joe pursed his lips. "Hm. Suppose we couldn't find it again?"

"Don't worry about that. I'll remember where I put it." Danny broke off. "Gosh," he said. "Look at that! Twin sharks!"

A short distance away, the surface of the sea was broken by the appearance of two black, triangular fins, about fifteen feet apart. As the boys watched, they sank into the water. Then all

at once the sea boiled, and out of the water sprang a monstrous black shape. It was more than twice as long as the raft and shaped like an immense bat, with a long, slender, whiplike tail. It seemed to flap its wings, the tips of which they had mistaken for sharks' fins, and then it fell back into the sea with a splash. The raft rocked.

"Holy smoke!" yelled Joe. "What is it?"

"Paddle!" Danny gasped. "Head for shore!"

They dug their paddles furiously into the water. But they were so frightened that at first the raft only turned round in place.

"Both together," cried Danny. "Get it in rhythm. If that thing comes up under us—"

They leaned far out and began to paddle in time, controlling their terror. At the same moment, not five feet away, the huge shape appeared

on the surface. It moved by flapping its wing-shaped fins in the water. They could see two horns and a kind of snout. The beast seemed to look at them, then it flapped lazily once or twice and submerged again.

"Easy," Danny said, although his voice shook. "Don't g-g-get scared. J-j-just paddle. Both together."

They made every stroke count. It was as if they were in a race, but a horrible one, for at any moment they expected the great fish to come up underneath them and smash them to bits. The shore came closer and closer.

"One more," Danny panted. *"And* one more. *And—"*

There was another tremendous splash behind them. Neither boy dared look. But the raft was shaken again, and then it was among the breakers. A wave caught it and rushed it forward. There was a ripping sound, and for an instant it seemed to stand still.

Then there came a rush of bubbles, and a loud hissing. The sides of the raft grew soft, and began to collapse. The boys made two or three more strokes and the raft sank beneath them.

They began to swim, frantically, not knowing if the monster was behind them—afraid to look.

Each time a wave crashed down upon them, they imagined they could feel the weight of the huge, bat-winged fish. But the breakers carried them in; they found themselves touching bottom, gasping and half drowned.

The Professor and Dr. Grimes came racing down the slope. They helped the boys further up the beach.

"Golly," said Joe, and for a moment could say nothing more.

"What was it, Professor?" Danny asked.

"It was a ray. Sometimes they're called devilfish. I don't think it would have harmed you except by accident. But it has a poisonous sting near the tail, and if it had come up under you—"

Danny shuddered. "Didn't it? Something ripped the raft."

"I think it was that spike of rock," said the Professor, pointing. "Remember, we almost hit it when we first came in. The tide was low then."

Dr. Grimes was shading his eyes, peering out to sea. He shook his head slowly. "No sign of the raft."

The Professor looked grave. "Now," he said, "we are really marooned."

CHAPTER TEN

Mud and an Idea

It was the morning of their fourth day on the island.

Danny awoke with the sun in his eyes and sat up, squinting. He shook Joe, who mumbled, "Right away, Ma," and rolled over.

"Get up," Danny whispered in his friend's ear.

Joe crawled sleepily out of the lean-to. "Wha' time is it?" he asked.

"Quarter after sunrise. Come on, let's have a swim before the men get up. If they see us in the ocean they'll start worrying. And as soon as they get up we'll have to start working."

The boys ran down the trail to the beach, threw off their pants, and dashed into the water. They swam about, now and then diving for colored shells or pebbles, but keeping within the safe arms of the bay. A row of sleepy iguanas watched them from the rocks, and numbers of birds—boobies, terns, and a few pelicans— squawked at them in a friendly fashion.

When they had finished their swim, they went

to gather eggs from the nests among the cliffs, and by the time they had returned the men were awake and had put fresh wood on the fire, which they always kept burning to save matches. They roasted the eggs among the hot ashes, along with some oysters, and finished up with bananas for dessert. Their dishes were some large, tough leaves, so that washing up was no problem. Then they gathered round the Professor, who had taken out the work sheet.

"To begin with," he said, "suppose we mark the day. Dan, will you notch the calendar?"

Danny opened his pocketknife and cut a notch in a stick planted in the ground before the lean-to.

"Number four," he said. "That makes it Wednesday."

"Good. Now for the day's schedule. Grimes, what about the radio?"

Dr. Grimes shook his head. "No luck yet. I can't understand how that crank could have been lost. I put the radio under cover that very first night, and I'm sure the crank was in it. Yet when we got up next morning, it was gone."

"We've been all over this," said the Professor. "It must have got loose, and when it fell off perhaps some animal took it."

"I've searched all over for it," Grimes said. "There's no trace of it."

Danny and Joe looked at each other. Almost imperceptibly Danny's eyelid drooped in a wink.

"Well," said Professor Bullfinch, "why don't you go on trying this morning to rig something?"

Dr. Grimes scowled. "I've been trying to make some sort of crank, but I can't manage without some way of fastening one on tightly."

"While you're doing that," said the Professor, "I'll gather seaweed for a salad, and try my luck at fishing. Those fat little fish the boys caught yesterday were delicious. I'll keep my eyes open for a turtle, too. They are excellent eating, and we can make good use of the shell. Danny and Joe—"

"We thought," Danny said, "that we might go into the forest and gather some more fruit. We made a special fruit carrier yesterday."

"Oh, yes. Well, has anyone any objections to this plan for the morning? No? Good. Now, that reminds me, Grimes. About our duel—"

"Have you changed your mind about it?"

"No. But it occurred to me that we ought to have some method of scoring. In our original idea, we were to be judged by Dr. Turbot and his associates. But here, we're all together on the same island, working as a group. We should

76

have some way of determining who has won when we get home."

"*If* we get home," Dr. Grimes amended, gloomily. "What's your scheme?"

"Perhaps the boys could make tally sticks, something like our calendar, and give us notches for each practical point we score."

"A good idea. Are the boys willing?"

Danny nodded. "We can get some sticks and carve them with your initials. Joe can keep Dr. Grimes's and I'll keep the Professor's."

Dr. Grimes's lips twitched in a smile as he looked at Joe. "It seems to me that I remember your writing me a poem," he said. "How did it go? 'My pal, Dr. Grimes.' I hope this won't give me an unfair advantage."

They all laughed. The Professor said, "I think I ought to get a small notch for the idea."

"Half a notch," said Grimes.

He went off to work on the transmitter, and Professor Bullfinch got out the fishing line and one of the empty K-ration boxes which he filled with mussels.

The boys took two spears from the back of the lean-to. They had made them the day before, after a pattern Danny remembered from a book. They were simply straight poles, the ends of which had been sharpened and then charred slowly in the fire until they were very hard. Then they got out the fruit carrier they had made. It consisted of two long wooden shafts, with two shorter ones lashed across them to make a square opening just large enough to accommodate the waterproof carton that had held K rations. This was held in place by a sling of cords that passed underneath it and were fastened to the poles.

They hung the canteens over their shoulders and took up the carrier. They went up the trail they had beaten to the forest.

As they ascended, the air grew warmer and damper. The thorn bushes gave way to tall green trees and thick underbrush. They crossed a grassy meadow where flowers made a colorful carpet, and bright green and yellow warblers and finches flew down to sing to them. Their trail ended at a ravine through which the stream flowed. Here bananas and guavas grew, and the slender, smooth-trunked papayas, the fruit of which was both delicious and nourishing. Soon the boys were busy filling their carrier.

Danny, pulling bananas down, said, "Now I understand the Professor saying last night that primitive people had to work hard just to stay alive."

Joe was clinging to the trunk of a papaya and

filling the front of his shirt with the melon-shaped fruit. He said, "You should have been here with Dr. Grimes and me that first day. I started to come down this very same tree and lost my hold. I slid all the way and landed right in that mud at the bottom."

Danny glanced at his friend. "Your mud coating is nearly worn off by now. You look—well—*almost* human."

"I just wasn't used to these trees," said Joe. Carefully, he began inching down the trunk. "It's like shinnying on a greased pole."

His feet touched the ground and he blew out a breath. "Whew! Believe me, I take my time now. I won't do that—ook!"

He had stepped on a slippery log and lost his balance. Wildly, he clutched at the air. He had just time to yell, "Help!" Then he fell face downward into the same puddle where he had fallen before.

Danny ran to help him and dragged him to his feet. "Are you hurt?" he stammered.

"Nope," said Joe. He raised one muddy arm and tried to wipe his face. "But look at me. Now I have to start all over again."

They rescued his papayas, and while Danny gathered some more fruit, Joe tried to wash himself off in the river, but without too much success.

Wildly he clutched at the air

When they returned to camp, the Professor was cleaning a string of varicolored fish. He looked at Joe with dismay.

"Not again, Joe," he said.

"It's getting to be a habit," grumbled Dr. Grimes. "And the lean-to is beginning to smell like a swamp."

The Professor took out his pipe. "We must really get busy making some soap," he observed. "I must say, Grimes, we thought of all sorts of basic things when we were planning the trip, but we forgot soap."

He examined Joe thoughtfully. "I wonder how sand would do?" he murmured.

"Nothing doing!" said Joe. "It would be like scrubbing with a file."

"Of course, if he could take a hot bath, it might help," said Grimes.

"Not in an oyster shell," the Professor said. He stuck his empty pipe in his mouth. "I wish I'd managed to save some tobacco. It's hard to think without it."

Danny was watching him fiddle with his pipe. He looked from the Professor to Joe, and suddenly he clapped his hands.

"I've got it!" Danny cried. "We'll make a pipeline!"

81

CHAPTER ELEVEN

The Crank Turns Up

The others stared at him. Then Joe said slowly, "How can we? We've only got the one pipe, and the Professor wouldn't want to give that up."

"Wait a minute," said the Professor. "Just what are you thinking of, Dan?"

"Well, the stream runs on the other side of that rocky ridge, no more than fifty paces from here."

"Go on."

"Why couldn't we chop the insides out of some rotten logs like the one Joe slipped on, or find some hollow logs, and pipe some water from the stream."

"Well? What then?"

"Then pipe it into a hole about three feet deep. When the hole's full of water, we put hot stones in it—"

"I see," said the Professor. "Like a Swedish bath. The stones would heat the water."

"Not bad," commented Dr. Grimes. "I'll vote for that. I could do with a good hot bath myself."

"Part of the history of human progress," said Professor Bullfinch, "is the development of comforts, such as the bathtub. We are advancing upward in the scale of history."

"Never mind that," said Dr. Grimes. "Let's get busy."

They set to work that very afternoon. They all went up into the forest, to begin with, to search for hollow logs. Near the marsh where Joe had fallen in, they found two that would do, and beyond the banana grove they found a fallen tree that was soft enough for them to gouge out the inside to make a long trough. They found pieces of obsidian and bound them to sticks to use as rough scrapers, and Joe found a curved branch and made a kind of hoe with a long piece of the glassy stone.

They pried the heavy logs out of the mud, using long poles as levers. They tied the nylon rope to the logs and hauled them away to the spot on the stream which they had selected.

This was a place where there was a little waterfall, no more than three feet high. They carefully propped up the scooped-out log so that one end of it was under the falling water, and arranged the other two logs to carry the water farther on, to the hole they dug.

The hole, which was about four feet square, gave them the greatest trouble. They could break the ground with sharp pointed sticks, but scooping the dirt out with nothing but large shells as shovels was a long, laborious process, and before it was over all of them had backaches.

The job took them three days to accomplish, for they had to spend a great deal of their time gathering food. They took turns fishing and collecting fruit and eggs. The boys practiced throwing their wooden spears every morning, and one day Joe, with a lucky cast, killed an iguana among the rocks. It was over three feet long, and a handsome gray-and-black color. They were, by then, so hungry for meat that they felt no squeamishness about eating lizard. As it turned out, when roasted the meat was stringy but quite good, tasting something like a cross between rabbit and chicken. After that they made it part of their regular diet.

When the pit was finished, and the bottom lined with smooth pieces of lava, they swung the trough into place under the waterfall. At first the water merely splashed all over the log without really filling it. After a few experiments, however, they found the right angle at which to set it, and soon a stream was flowing down through the pipeline and their improvised bathtub began to fill up.

They all stood round and watched it, grinning at each other.

"It was quite a job," said Professor Bullfinch. "But getting it done makes you feel good, doesn't it?"

"There's one thing we forgot," Joe said. "We ought to have a drainpipe."

"We won't really need one," said Dr. Grimes. "We can cut a shallow trench at one side, where the ground slopes toward the cliff. Then, when we're through bathing, we let the water run in again until all the dirty water has been replaced."

"Good. Now let's get a fireplace ready to heat the stones in," said the Professor.

It was the work of only a few minutes to build a second, circular fireplace close to the bathtub. They brought a burning branch up from their camp and started a fire, and when it was blazing they began piling smooth stones in it. When the stones were hot, they would be rolled the short distance to the bathub.

"I never thought I'd go to so much trouble to wash my face," Danny chuckled, as they were searching about for stones of the proper size.

"I'll remember this next time Mom tells me to wash behind my ears."

He stopped, white-faced, and stood up. For a terrible thought had come to him, even as he said those words.

"Joe!" he said softly. "It just occurred to me. All this time we've been missing. Do you suppose our folks think we're dead?"

Joe straightened. "Golly! That's right."

Danny rubbed his forehead. "I never thought of it when we hid the crank of the radio. But I'll bet they think we drowned. *I* know I'm alive, so I just didn't think that anybody else would think I *wasn't*."

"Danny! We better return that crank."

"But—oh, you're right, Joe."

Before he could say another word, there was a shout from Dr. Grimes. "Look at this, Bullfinch! Look what I've found!"

They all hurried over to see. Dr. Grimes was holding up a curiously shaped piece of stone.

"I pulled that rock out of the sand, and under it found this thing," he explained. "Do you recognize it?"

"Why, it's a stone axhead, or hammer head," said Professor Bullfinch.

"You mean there are other castaways like us on this island?" Joe cried.

"Not castaways, Joe," the Professor smiled. "There may be natives who work in stone."

"Not at all," Dr. Grimes said, pressing his lips together.

"Why not?"

"I am certain this island is uninhabited. In the first place, we've been here for more than a week. Surely, if there were natives they would have investigated the smoke from our fires."

"Maybe they're shy," Danny suggested.

"In the second place, the birds and animals have obviously never seen men before."

"Perhaps the men haven't harmed them," said the Professor.

"Nonsense! And in the third place, the Galapagos Islands are known to be uninhabited."

"But, Grimes, we may not be on one of the Galapagos Islands," the Professor objected. "Perhaps we're on a remote island near the chain, but one that has not yet been discovered. It might be better to withhold judgment until all the facts are in."

"It's as unlikely as that there is life on Mars," Dr. Grimes said firmly. "Look at this axhead.

Why, it was obviously made in the Late Stone Age. I judge it to be at least ten thousand years old."

Danny said, "Anyway, there's no reason why we can't use it. Our obsidian axhead is beginning to be too chipped to use."

The Professor began poking in the sand with a stick. "If we search about," he began, "we may come upon some other evidence—"

Danny said nervously, "Farther up the hill might be a good place to look. . . ."

He broke off. The Professor was picking a small object out of the sand.

"I've found something already!" crowed Professor Bullfinch.

"Head of a war club!" Dr. Grimes said authoritatively. "Late Stone Age?"

"I'm afraid not," said the Professor. "Early Atomic Age."

Danny and Joe turned pale. The Professor was holding the missing crank of the emergency radio.

CHAPTER TWELVE

The Water Wheel

"It must have dropped off," said the Professor. "Then as we walked about we kicked sand over it—"

Danny took a deep breath. "No, Professor," he said, forcing the words out. "I buried it there."

"And I helped him," Joe blurted.

Professor Bullfinch stared from one to the other. "But—but I don't understand," he said. "Why on earth—?"

"I thought," Danny said miserably, "that it would be fun to stay here for a while."

"It was my fault just as much as his," Joe said.

"Fun? But—"

"It's perfectly clear," Dr. Grimes snapped. "Boys have no sense whatever. They were thinking only of the adventure."

"Didn't you realize," Professor Bullfinch asked in a gentle voice, "that your parents would be worried sick?"

"No, Professor," Danny said. "To be honest,

we didn't till just a few minutes ago. I—I guess I just acted without stopping to think. But we were going to get it back today. Honestly we were. It was only when Dr. Grimes found that stone ax that we were sidetracked."

The Professor sighed. "It was a foolish thing to do, my boy," he said. "However, there is never any point in crying over what's past."

"I think they deserve a severe punishment," said Dr. Grimes.

"Perhaps now that they know what a mistake they made, it's punishment enough."

"I don't agree. I think they should be made to operate the transmitter all day today. That will help make up for the week we've lost."

"We haven't exactly lost the week," the Professor said. "We've all learned a good deal, and knowledge can't be counted lost time. However, perhaps you're right. It won't hurt the boys to act as radiomen for one day. Tomorrow we can go back on our hourly schedule. Do you agree, boys?"

The two nodded silently.

They took the waterproof cover off the transmitter and replaced the crank. There was a tiny setscrew that held it in place, and Professor Bullfinch asked, "How did you manage to unscrew this? Have you a screwdriver, Dan?"

"No. But remember what you said about the different uses for the same tool? I used the point of my smallest knife blade."

He tightened the little screw and experimentally turned the crank. After a few seconds the light glowed dimly.

"Very well," said Professor Bullfinch. "Grimes, you and I will be food gatherers this afternoon, and we'll also be the first to take hot baths. The boys can bathe tonight."

"Get busy, you two," growled Dr. Grimes. "Let's hope there's a ship steaming within hearing distance."

The two men walked back up the hill and began rolling hot stones into the water. A cloud of steam arose, and they tossed a coin to see who would wash first. Meantime, Danny sat down and strapped the transmitter between his legs. He began cranking without a word.

He and Joe took it in turn, fifteen minutes at a stretch. During one of his rest periods, as he was rubbing his hands to get the cramp out of them, Danny said, "The thing I hate is wasting time this way."

"It won't be a waste of time if they find us," said Joe.

"I know that. I mean, we could be exploring the island, or making things we need."

"Now, Danny. Don't start anything that means trouble again," Joe wailed. "We got into enough hot water—I mean, we didn't get into the hot water—well, you know what I mean."

"Yes. But if there was some way of working this thing mechanically. . . ."

"How could we do that?"

"I don't know," Danny said, shaking his head. "But I'm going to think about it."

"All right," said Joe. "And I'm going to hope you don't get any ideas."

By midafternoon it became clear that the boys' strength was running out, and the two men relented and took over the transmitter. The boys went for a swim to refresh themselves, and after that they felt so relaxed that they couldn't face the labor of heating stones, so they decided to let the hot bath go until the next day. But Danny spent a long time staring at the pipeline and then at the waterfall which fed it.

At dinner he said abruptly, "Professor Bullfinch, I've been wondering whether there isn't some way of turning the handle of the transmitter by water power."

The Professor calmly finished the mouthful he was eating. Then he said, "My boy, you constantly surprise me. I suppose it's only natural. I sometimes forget how full of ideas I was at your age. I guess it's possible, but it would be difficult."

"But then we could keep the transmitter going all day long, and still be free to work," Danny said, persuasively. "I've been thinking about it. We'd need a water wheel."

"Yes."

"We could move the transmitter over to the other side of the rocks. The stream falls about twenty feet over the cliffs, there, to a shelf above the sea. There's just room to set up a water wheel and get the full force of the fall."

"What would you make paddles out of?" asked Dr. Grimes. "Tree trunks?"

"No. The emergency chest. It's plywood. We might be able to split it up with the stone ax and the raft knife."

"Hmm. And I suppose we could make the axle out of a good, straight pole. We'd have to drill holes, though," said the Professor.

"Maybe I can help with that," Dr. Grimes said, beginning to be interested. "I used to know how to make a bow-drill with a couple of sticks, a nail, and some string. Among all the junk in your pockets, Danny, do you have a nail?"

"Sure. I always carry a couple."

Danny took out a pencil and a scrap of paper. "Look, here's how we could make the wheel.

The water turns the paddles, which are fastened to an axle. The axle turns a round disk, and the crank handle is fastened to the outer edge of the disk so that as the wheel goes round it turns the crank."

"What could we use for the disk?" asked the Professor. "That would be the most difficult, because it would have to be an exact circle."

"I've thought of that, too. The round door on the front of the radio, the one that holds the antenna reel, is just the right size. There's only a cotter pin holding it in place, and when we take the antenna reel off there'll be a hole in the center just right for the shaft to go through."

"Excellent!" said Professor Bullfinch. "What do you say, Grimes?"

Dr. Grimes stroked his chin. "It helps make up for their foolish prank," he admitted.

The Professor raised a canteen. "To the success of the water wheel," he said. "And it's only right that we should drink the toast in water!"

The very next morning, after breakfast, they began work on it. It proved more difficult than they had expected, but they were all excited by the idea and worked hard.

To begin with, it took over an hour to split part of the plywood box into six pieces, about five inches wide and eighteen inches long. They drilled holes in the ends of these pieces, and in the ends of pairs of thin poles. Then they whittled wooden pegs, and hammered them into the holes, to make six sets of paddles.

These paddles were then fixed into holes in a perfectly straight, tough wooden shaft, which in turn was connected to the circular door from the front of the transmitter. Lastly, the crank handle was fastened firmly to the outside edge of this disk, using parts from the antenna reel to hold it. The radio was strapped between two upright posts driven deep into the ground.

The wooden shaft rested on two forked sticks, one on each side of the falling water. The Professor brought some iguana fat and greased these forks and the axle also. Then the wheel was set in place and the axle connected to the crank handle.

Slowly, the wheel began to turn, creaking a

little. Instead of lashings, they had drilled holes and pounded in wooden pegs to hold the parts together, and they watched anxiously, hoping the machine wouldn't fall apart. Danny helped it along by turning it once or twice.

Water splashed from the edges of the paddles. More and more swiftly the wheel turned. They all fidgeted, biting their fingernails or holding their breaths with impatience.

Suddenly the light on the radio flickered, weakly at first, then more brightly. It began blinking, three longs, three shorts, three longs.

"We're transmitting," the Professor said, drawing a relieved breath.

He took off his glasses, and rubbed his eyes. "Water power," he mused. "We have come slowly up the scale of man's achievements, from the stone ax to the bathtub, and now—the water wheel. And all in a little more than a week."

CHAPTER THIRTEEN

"I Shot an Arrow . . ."

Their ninth day on the island was a day to be remembered. To begin with, there was the finding of the turtle.

The boys ran down, as usual, to have their swim in the morning. They had all been so tired the night before, after the building of the water mill, that they had once again put off the job of heating water. Their hard work had made them grimy, and they plunged into the sea with delight. Danny scrubbed himself with handfuls of sand. Joe, however, complained that he was too ticklish for such treatment, and since he was dirtier than Danny he'd have to scrub harder. He contented himself with just swimming.

When they had dried themselves in the sun, they started off for one of the rocky arms that guarded their beach, to hunt for birds' eggs. At the end of the beach they both stopped short. An enormous sea turtle was lying among the rocks.

It was a great, green beast, a full three feet long and much too heavy for the boys to move out of the rocks. Something had attacked it and wounded it. It must have reached the shallows where its enemy could not follow. There it had died and had been washed up on the shore.

The boys ran to fetch Professor Bullfinch and Dr. Grimes. When the two men had come to the beach, they were able to drag the turtle down to the sand.

"This is a stroke of luck," said the Professor. His eyes grew dreamy. "Turtle soup, turtle steaks. . . ."

"But is it all right to eat it?" Danny asked. "After all, it died of a wound."

Professor Bullfinch smiled. "Most of the meat we normally eat dies of a wound," he replied. "As long as it is fresh and clean, as this is from the sea, there's nothing wrong with eating it."

"It'll be quite a job cutting it up and cleaning it," Dr. Grimes said. "However, it should be worth it."

With their knives and stone axes they went to work on the creature. After several hours they succeeded in getting most of the meat and almost a hundred round, tough-skinned eggs that looked like golf balls, and could be bounced without breaking. They emptied out the shell, which was smooth and leathery, and brought it up to their camp to dry. Then they feasted on the rich steaks which, when broiled, were delicious. They ate some of the eggs, too, and found them not much tastier than real golf balls might have been.

After they had dined, the men lay down for a nap and the boys, taking some turtle fat with them, went to check on the water wheel. They had found that they could not allow the wheel to run steadily, as the friction of the wooden axle against its forked supports would have been too great no matter how much they greased it. They therefore let it run for half-hour periods with long rests in between, during which they cranked the transmitter by hand. The boys had taken on the duty of keeping the mill greased and moving it in and out of the waterfall.

They got it started, made sure it was sending out its signal, and then clambered up the rocks and sat down in the sun. From their perch, they could look along the coast. Blacks cliffs fell away into the sea; they were not high but very steep, and above them the ground sloped more gradually upward to the peak of the extinct volcano near the center of the island.

The boys were almost drowsing. Suddenly, Danny sat up straight. "What's that?" he exclaimed, pointing.

Joe opened his eyes. "Where?"

Danny stood up, squinting against the glare of the sun on the sea. He pointed at the spot where the coast bent away out of sight. A large dark rock jutted into the water, and at the top of it, growing in no more than a handful of soil, stood a single bent, gnarled tree.

"I thought I saw something move there. It looked like—like a man."

"Probably some animal," said Joe, lazily.

"No, I'm sure it was a man. It was doing something at that tree, and then it ran off."

"A monkey."

"Professor Bullfinch said there aren't any monkeys in this region."

"Well, Dr. Grimes said there aren't any men in this region, so we're even."

Danny grabbed his friend's arm. "Come on," he said. "Let's investigate."

Joe groaned. "Why? If there are any natives on this island, they're probably cannibals. And I don't feel up to being anybody's dinner."

Danny started off. "Okay," he called, "you stay here. I'm going."

"Oh, shucks! Wait a minute. I may as well go along to keep you out of trouble. Not that it'll do any good. . . ."

They crossed the stream higher up, and then

100

"Let's investigate."

returned to the edge of the cliffs where the ground was more open. They plodded along for ten or fifteen minutes, stumbling over broken lava, and now and then making a detour to avoid a particularly thick clump of cactus. At last they came to the summit of the large rock and stood beneath the twisted tree.

Joe said, "How could we tell if anybody's been here? This rock doesn't hold any footprints."

"Don't look down," said Danny. "Look up."

"Up? Do you expect them to leave footprints in the air?"

"Don't be silly! I mean *that*."

Joe followed Danny's pointing finger. Then he gulped. High above their heads, stuck fast in the wood, was a long arrow.

"Holy smoke!" said Joe. "Indians!"

Danny stared eagerly at the arrow. "Looks like he shot his arrow and it went too high. He couldn't reach it, and he couldn't climb the tree because of those."

"Those" were thorns, almost three inches long, that protruded from the tree trunk at intervals.

"You mean he went to get help?" said Joe. "And that means he'll be coming back soon. With more arrows.... Good-bye!"

"Wait a sec. You know how the Professor is always talking about getting the facts. If we go back without any proof they won't believe us. Let's get that arrow."

"But Dan, I don't like thorns either," Joe cried. He kept looking about him as if that unknown archer might suddenly appear from behind a cactus plant.

"We don't have to climb. You weigh less than I do. Get up on my shoulders."

"But—but—but—oh, okay."

Danny bent over next to the tree. Joe knelt on his back, then slowly stood up, wobbling a bit. Danny straightened. Both boys braced themselves with their hands against the tree trunk, being careful to avoid the thorns.

Joe took hold of the arrow and pulled. It had a head made of bone, and it was so firmly embedded in the wood that he had to cut around it with his pocketknife to get it free. Then, cautiously, he got down.

"All right," he said. "Now you've got it, let's go."

They started out walking, but before long they were trotting and then running, their thoughts on the unknown men somewhere behind them. They took a short cut higher up the slope to avoid

103

the cactus, and splashed through the stream at a shallow place. They rushed down to the camp and then took the trail to the beach.

The two men were standing around something that simmered and bubbled over a fire, and gave off a dreadful smell. They looked up as the boys came panting into view, and the Professor said with a broad smile, "I have a surprise for you. Grimes and I have been making soap. Isn't that wonderful?"

"We've got a surprise for *you,*" Danny gasped. "Look at this."

"Oh, you made an arrow? How clever. But our soap—"

"We didn't make it, Professor. We found it in a tree."

"Growing there?" said the Professor, with a puzzled look. Then his expression changed. "You mean there are natives on this island?"

"Impossible! Let me see that," Dr. Grimes snapped, taking the arrow.

Both men bent over it. "There's no question of it," Professor Bullfinch said. "It is newly made. Look at the feathers, and the sinew that holds the head to the shaft."

"I'm afraid you're right," said Dr. Grimes. "This may mean trouble."

"Oh, not necessarily," the Professor was beginning, when Danny suddenly said, "Trouble? Oh, gosh! I just remembered something!"

"Oh, yes, our soap," said the Professor mildly. "Yes, we took wood ashes and turtle fat and cooked them in the turtle shell. I think it was rather brilliant of us. Grimes and I should both get the credit for it. It was his idea to smear the shell with clay, to keep it from—"

"I don't mean your soap," said Danny impatiently. "I mean the water wheel. We forgot all about it."

Without another word, he darted back up the trail. The others followed, still not quite sure what he meant. They climbed over the hump of rocks, but even before they descended to the shore the reason for Danny's haste became evident. A thread of gray smoke was rising from the base of the cliff. They scrambled down the tumbled lava blocks to the shore. Here, at the foot of the high waterfall, they had put their paddle wheel.

It was clear at a glance what had happened. The wooden shaft, turning on its wooden supports, had grown hotter and hotter from friction in the long interval while the boys had been away. At last it had burst into flame.

The wheel still turned, for the water had kept it from burning. But at the other end, the shaft had burned right to the radio. The metal case was smudged with black, although it did not appear to be harmed. But when they had loosened the screws and removed the face plate, they saw that the heat had cracked tubes and fused connections. The radio would never send another call for help.

CHAPTER FOURTEEN

Dr. Grimes Springs His Trap

"We can't honestly blame you boys," Professor Bullfinch said, as they surveyed the ruin. "After all, it was immensely important to learn that we are not alone on this island."

"They should have reported to us before rushing off like that," Dr. Grimes said sternly. "Danny's always doing thoughtless, headstrong things."

"Come now, Grimes," the Professor said soothingly. "I'm sure when you were younger you weren't much different. In any case, there's nothing we can do about the radio except hope that someone has picked up our signal. But there *is* something we can do about our neighbors."

"You're right about that," said Grimes. "We can prepare to defend ourselves."

"Oh, I didn't mean that. I meant that we could visit them."

At this, Dr. Grimes turned perfectly purple.

"You dreamer! You visionary!" he exclaimed. "Visit them? We'll undoubtedly have them visit us before long—with their butcher knives ready. Why don't you just sprinkle yourself with parsley and lie down on a plate?"

"Well, chiefly because we haven't any parsley," said the Professor gently. "Come, now, Grimes. We have no proof that these people are unfriendly. And we certainly have no proof that they're cannibals."

"Proof?" Dr. Grimes controlled himself with an effort. "Bullfinch, I have no intention of waiting to be put into a pot for proof. They may be friendly. But why should we take chances? When that man returns and finds his arrow gone, he'll know we're here—if they don't already know it, and haven't just been biding their time. We must make weapons. And we must surround the camp with traps so they can't come on us at night, without warning."

Professor Bullfinch tapped the stem of his pipe against his teeth. "Well," he said at last, "I suppose there's some sense in that. What do you boys think?"

"What's the difference what *they* think?" Dr. Grimes snapped.

"We're all in this together, Grimes," the Professor replied. "If they're to be eaten with us, they should vote with us. Well, boys?"

"I vote to be prepared," said Danny.

"So do I—and I don't mean as a dish," said Joe.

They began by making two more spears, like those the boys already had. Then they cut some shorter sticks and fastened chunks of stone into clefts at one end of them to make a kind of rude war club. The boys cut quantities of thorny branches, and piled them along the ridge of rock, leaving a narrow entranceway so that they could go for water.

Dr. Grimes had been drawing diagrams on a bit of paper. "I have developed a man trap," he said, "which we can set at night. Come with me. I'll demonstrate it."

He found a tall, springy sapling growing beside their trail to the banana grove. Using some of the nylon rope, he made a large noose and fastened it to the top of the young tree. Then he bent the tree down and pegged the lower part of the noose to the ground with two wooden hooks.

"Anyone running along this trail," he explained, "will hit the lower edge of the noose. The pegs will jerk out, and the noose will close on him and hoist him up."

"Isn't that rather drastic?" the Professor remarked. "It might kill a native, and we're really not at war with them."

"Not at all. It can't really hurt anyone," Dr. Grimes returned. "As you can see, it is tripped in such a way that it closes around the body and holds a man helpless."

"Very ingenious," said the Professor. "How did you ever happen to think of such a thing?"

"Why, I—er—" Dr. Grimes reddened. Then he said, "To tell the truth, I read about it in a book called *Simba, the Jungle Lad,* when I was eleven years old."

Joe scratched his head. "I don't know whether we ought to give Dr. Grimes a notch, or give it to Simba instead," he grinned.

"Oh, let's not be fussy," said the Professor. "Give it to your pal, Dr. Grimes."

They made two more of these traps on the hill slope. Then Joe cut an elaborate notch in the doctor's tally stick.

Dinner was a rather quiet meal, for they were all busy with their own thoughts, chiefly about the islanders. What kind of people would they be? Were they cannibals, or would they be gentle and timid?

Danny was even more silent than the others, for he could not escape feeling that it was all in some way his fault. He so often acted without thinking first. Professor Bullfinch had told him many times that this was not how a scientist

110

should behave, and he always made good resolves never to do it again. But somehow an exciting idea would occur to him, or a situation would arise that seemed terribly interesting, and he would find himself plunging into action without a thought for the consequences.

And here was another instance. If he hadn't rushed off so heedlessly, they would still have their radio. And if he hadn't taken the arrow, the natives might never have known they were on the island. He groaned within himself, and looked at his wooden spear and club. What good would makeshift weapons like these do against a hundred howling, hungry savages?

When they all went to bed, he couldn't sleep but tossed and turned until Joe grumbled and begged him to settle down. Danny slipped out of the lean-to and sat by the fire, wishing he could think of some way out of the mess. Thoughts of his mother came to him, too: her merry smile and warm look haunted him, and he felt more guilty than ever. If he hadn't been so selfish and thoughtless, if he'd never hidden the crank, they might have been rescued long ago.

He sighed, and put another stick of wood on the fire. Sometimes it was hard to know what was best. Sometimes a thing looked right until you saw it from someone else's point of view.

He got up restlessly, and decided to check on the traps before going to bed. After all, some small animal might have sprung one of them.

He took his spear and the flashlight, which had been part of the raft supplies, and walked softly up the trail that led to the banana grove. The moon, almost full, made a silvery lacework of the leaves, and below him the ocean hissed black and silver against the white sand of the beach. From the marsh he could hear strange peeps and chuckles, and the calls of night birds.

From time to time he switched the light on and off, to make certain of the trail. He came to the trap and almost stepped into it, for the pale nylon rope was almost the same color as the moonlight. He stood for a moment playing his light about. All was silent and safe.

Then, without warning, he heard from the direction of the camp a loud bellow.

His first thought was that it was an animal, although they had seen nothing large enough to make such a noise. But as he started back, at a run, he could distinguish words: "Up! Up! They're attacking!"

The voice was that of Dr. Grimes. The hair rose on Danny's neck and he froze, gripping his spear tightly.

"This way!" he heard Dr. Grimes call. The voice seemed, now, to come from his right, higher up the hill. He remembered that there was another trap up there. He swung round and started for it.

Cactus tore at his legs but he never heeded the scratches. Directly ahead of him he heard a crashing in the brush. There was a loud, blood-curdling yell that almost made his heart stop.

He faltered, took a breath, and ran on. A shadowy figure loomed up ahead of him. He dodged and raised his spear.

"Help!" the figure shouted.

"Joe?" Danny called.

"Who's that? Danny? Where are you? Is it you?"

"It's me." Danny could see his friend's face now, in the moonlight. Joe was carrying one of the war clubs.

"Come on," Danny said. "They must be up at the trap."

They ran on together. A little way behind them they heard someone panting up the hill. They came to the trap. A dark shape was dangling a foot or two off the ground, twisting and swinging violently as it struggled.

Danny caught Joe by the arm. The leaves and

113

A dark shape was dangling

fronds all about them made it difficult to see clearly.

"Get your club ready," Danny said. He balanced his own spear in his hand, and then flashed the light on.

"Gosh!" Joe breathed. "A native."

Then he said, "And he looks just like Dr. Grimes!"

"Get me down from here!" the native roared.

"He talks English!" said Joe. "And he sounds like Dr. Grimes, too."

"I've got news for you," said Danny.

Then, as a relief from the tension of the moments before, he began to laugh helplessly.

CHAPTER FIFTEEN

Smoke on the Water

Fortunately, the noose had caught Dr. Grimes about the waist and the only injury he suffered was to his dignity. Professor Bullfinch came up, panting, and they cut the rope and helped Dr. Grimes to the ground.

When he could catch his breath, Dr. Grimes said, "I heard something moving up here. I know I did."

The Professor made a throat-clearing noise. They could not see his expression, but his voice sounded amused, as he said, "It seems to me, Grimes, that you acted hastily, charging up here. One might almost call it—er—headstrong."

"I—" Dr. Grimes began.

"Yes, indeed. You didn't wait until you had all the facts, but leaped at once to conclusions."

"I—" said Dr. Grimes again.

"What would you say, Danny?" asked the Professor.

"Yes," Danny replied, in a very small voice.

The rest of the night passed without incident.

In the morning they breakfasted on turtle meat, bananas, and oysters. Then they gathered round the Professor, as was their custom.

"Mark the calendar, Dan," the Professor said.

"This is our tenth day," Danny said, as he cut the notch. "Tuesday."

"Happy Tuesday," said Joe, mournfully.

Professor Bullfinch looked at their disturbed faces. "Come, cheer up," he said. "We aren't soup—yet. Let me see, since our duel is still going on, I think Dr. Grimes deserves a notch for his invention of the man-trap."

"I've already made it," Joe said. "But—well, you know, I wouldn't say anything against Dr. Grimes, but I think he ought to have it taken away from him for falling into his own trap. That wasn't very practical."

Dr. Grimes opened his mouth and then closed it again. Then he said, "Traitor!"

"I'm afraid he's right, though," the Professor chuckled. "Half a notch, anyway."

"Oh, I'll remember about it."

"All right. Now, let's discuss our situation. Shall we try to communicate with the natives?"

"I'm against that," said Dr. Grimes. "I think we ought to stay close to camp today. If they're really peaceful, they may try to visit us. If they aren't peaceful—they may visit us anyway. In either case, I think we ought to be near our base."

"Yes, that's sensible," the Professor agreed. "What do you think, boys?"

The two nodded, although Danny did so reluctantly, for he could not help feeling that perhaps the Professor was right and they had nothing to fear from the natives. On the other hand, he remembered Robinson Crusoe's experiences: the grisly cannibal feasts, and Crusoe's narrow escape from death. Perhaps it was best not to take chances.

Later that morning, as the two scientists were preparing the last of the turtle meat for lunch and cleaning some fish they had caught, Joe and Danny came slowly to the fire, smiling sheepishly, with their hands behind their backs.

"We've brought you each a present," Danny announced.

"Another arrow?" Dr. Grimes asked, suspiciously.

"No, nothing like that," Danny giggled.

From behind them, he and Joe drew out two objects. One was a flute, made from a hollow reed with holes carefully cut in it. The other was an odd-looking instrument: its body was the case of the emergency radio, emptied of all its parts. A neck made of wood was stuck in the hole at the top where the crank had been. It had three strings, two of twisted gut and one of thin wire.

"We thought," Joe said shyly, "that maybe these would help cheer you up."

The scientists looked at each other. Then they took the instruments.

"Thank you, boys. Thank you very much," said the Professor.

Dr. Grimes coughed, to hide his emotion. "When did you make them?"

"This morning. Since we weren't gathering fruit and had to stick around, we thought we ought to do something for you. To sort of show you how grateful we are for—for everything."

"Well, I—I'm sure both Dr. Grimes and I owe a great deal to you, too," said the Professor. "Hem! Grimes, let's have a little music."

Dr. Grimes blew experimentally into his flute. "Not bad," he said, raising his eyebrows. "Not bad at all."

"Since there's no bow, I'll have to play this like a guitar," Professor Bullfinch said. He tightened the strings, plucking at them, his head on one side.

The instruments were not exactly in tune, nor were they precisely lovely in tone, for the guitar sounded like a sick bullfrog and the flute a little like an hysterical steam whistle. But the four made no complaint. To them, the simple melodies sounded delightful, and the two men were as pleased with their presents as if they were children at Christmas.

When at last they stopped, laughing together over a particularly loud discord, Professor Bullfinch said, "Ah, this reminds me, my dear Grimes, of that evening on which you first challenged me to a duel of desert islands."

"Humph!" grunted Dr. Grimes. "If I had known what it was going to lead to, I'd have kept my mouth shut."

"It has been a most interesting vacation, all the same," said the Professor, stroking his bristling chin. "And as an experiment, most rewarding. Still, I think I prefer the laboratory."

"There's such a thing as being *too* practical," Dr. Grimes said.

"Well, I think a desert island is fine," said Joe. "As long as you don't have to be on one."

"Almost anything is fine as long as it isn't forced on you," the Professor said. "Just imagine how terrible it would be if someone *made* you eat chocolate cake, even when you were full and didn't want any more."

"I'm imagining," said Joe dreamily. "Go on. Tell me more."

They all laughed. Professor Bullfinch idly

plucked the strings, and said, "Music is supposed to have charms to soothe the savage breast. I wonder whether we ought to march on the natives playing these instruments?"

"I'm afraid it would only enrage them," Grimes snorted.

"Well, Danny," said the Professor, "you've been very quiet. A penny for your thoughts."

Danny had been gazing out to sea. He started at the Professor's words, and said, "I was just wondering whether there was something wrong with my eyes."

"Eh? Why should there be?"

"Take a look out there."

They all turned to stare at the ocean. A smudge of black smoke was visible on the horizon.

"Not a thing," said Joe. "Except I guess somebody's burning leaves out there, or something."

Then he choked. "Burning?" he cried. "On the ocean? Hey!"

"You're right!" the Professor said, jumping to his feet. "It's smoke. That can only mean one thing—"

"A ship!" shouted Dr. Grimes. And in a lower voice, full of tension, he added, "but—is she headed this way?"

CHAPTER SIXTEEN

The Vanishing of Joe

They all stood motionless, straining their eyes to watch the smoke.   They hardly dared breathe.

After fifteen minutes Danny said, "I think it's getting closer."

"Ssh!" hissed Dr. Grimes, as if silence would help him see better.

But another quarter hour of waiting left no doubt: the ship was actually coming nearer.   She was still many miles away, but the column of smoke was larger and beneath it they could now make out a tiny dark speck that must be the superstructure of the ship herself.

Dr. Grimes grabbed a blazing stick from the fire.   "Now or never!" he cried.   He plunged up the hill, to the signal fire he had prepared on the ledge against just such a moment as this.   He thrust the torch into it.   The dry, thorny branches began crackling, and within minutes a tall column of smoke rose high in the air.

They watched the ship.

"Look!" Danny shouted, all at once.

Unmistakably, a spark of red shot up from the ship.

"A rocket," said the Professor. "They've seen our signal!"

"Yippee!" Joe yelled, unable to contain himself any longer. "We're saved!"

"I dislike jumping to conclusions," said Professor Bullfinch, "but in this case the hypothesis may be correct. *Hooray!*"

And with that, he seized Dr. Grimes's hands and began a wild dance of triumph. Dr. Grimes's sour face was split with a wide grin that made him look like a completely different man. Danny and Joe capered madly around the two scientists.

After a few moments they were able to quiet down, and the Professor said, "Let us collect our things. We'll want to save our stone tools and our musical instruments as souvenirs. And let's all make ourselves presentable. It is," he added, "a point of honor with me that when they pick us up we shouldn't look like beachcombers. After all, we've managed very well so far."

Dr. Grimes nodded. He looked at Joe and said, "I think it might be a good idea, Bullfinch, if the boys took a bath. We haven't yet had a chance to try out the soap."

A tall column of smoke rose in the air

"By George, that's right! And after you and I went to so much trouble to make it!"

"But, Professor!" Danny protested. "I'm clean."

"I'd hardly go so far as to say 'clean.' You are less dirty than Joe, who—I'm sorry to say—looks and smells more like a swamp cabbage than a boy."

"But we can get washed on the ship," said Joe.

"Have you no pride at all?" Dr. Grimes said severely.

"No," Joe replied.

"Well, we have enough for both of you. We'll make a fire and you can start some stones heating. Bullfinch, you get some soap."

The Professor took one of the K-ration containers—which they found constantly useful—and went down to the beach. In the turtle shell, which they had taken off the fire, there was a small quantity of a rather gluey substance. It had a peculiar greenish color and smelled of turtle, but it was undeniably soap of a sort. Professor Bullfinch scooped some of it into the container and handed it to Danny.

In the excitement of their anticipated rescue, they had forgotten completely about the natives. They ran up to the hole they had dug for a bath-

126

tub, and moved the trough at the stream so that the hole could fill with fresh water. They soon had stones heating in a large fire, while down below, at the camp, the two men built up their fire to act as a signal to the ship.

"Gee, won't it be swell to be home again?" Joe said.

"You bet. And won't the other kids be jealous?"

"I don't care. I'm just going to eat. I'll start with roast beef and mashed potatoes, and then fried chicken, and ice cream . . ." Joe sighed. "There's only one drawback to this rescue business," he added.

"What's that?"

"Using this soap. Do we have to?"

"Tell you what," said Danny. "I'll let you have the honor of being the first to try it."

"Are you kidding?" Joe got to his feet. "That stuff will probably burn our skin off."

"Well, that's one way of getting clean. Come on, Joe. Don't be a coward."

"But I *am* a coward."

Danny snatched up the container. "Just a little dab of it," he cooed. "If it doesn't eat through your hands, we'll know it's all right."

"Not me." Joe dodged away.

Laughing, Danny went for him. Joe ducked, and stuck out a foot. Danny went sprawling. In a flash Joe recovered, laughing in his turn, and darted up the hill. He disappeared between the trees.

Danny picked himself up and recovered the container. He ran after his friend, yelling, "Joe! It won't hurt. Come and take your bath!"

He was a little slowed by his own laughter. He entered the forest, and suddenly he stopped. Something was wrong, and for a moment he couldn't put his finger on what it was. Then it

came to him: the quiet. It was *too* quiet. The usual friendly birds were silent, nor were there any other noises—no frogs, no rustlings in the underbrush.

"Joe," he called. "Come on out, Joe. I promise I won't. . . ."

His voice trailed away before that all-enveloping silence.

He walked a few paces. Then he stood still again, every nerve on the stretch, his spine tingling.

In the soft earth there were fresh footprints—the prints of many large, naked feet.

CHAPTER SEVENTEEN

"After Them!"

For an instant, Danny was stunned. Then he pulled himself together and began to search about for further evidences of what had happened.

Mixed with the prints of bare feet were the marks of Joe's sneakers. All the footprints led away toward the banana grove. Danny followed them for a few yards, and at the base of a tree he found a crumpled, dirty piece of cloth: a handkerchief which Joe had obviously dropped to show which way he was being taken.

Danny fought down an impulse to go on after his friend. "This time," he said to himself, "I won't be headstrong."

He turned and ran as fast as he could, back toward the camp.

The Professor and Dr. Grimes were folding up the blanket between them, as he came pelting down the hill.

"Hold still, Bullfinch," Dr. Grimes was saying. He lifted his head, and called to Danny, "What's the matter? Water too hot?"

Danny gulped for air. "The natives!" he cried. "They've got Joe!"

"What!"

They dropped the blanket. Dr. Grimes grabbed Danny by one arm, and Professor Bullfinch took him by the other.

"Look out," he said. "You'll pull me in half. Joe ran up into the jungle. We were playing. When I went after him he was gone, and I found footprints all over the place. Big ones, of bare feet. They took him toward the banana grove."

"Great heavens!" exclaimed the Professor. "It's my fault. I should never have let you two go up to the bathtub alone."

"It's much more my fault," Dr. Grimes said somberly. "I was the one who proposed it. I should have thought—"

"No point in our competing for guilt," Professor Bullfinch cut in. "We must go after him."

"But the ship—?"

They all turned to look at the sea. By now the distant ship was visible, although still too far away for details to be seen.

"They may not be here for another hour," said the Professor. "We can't wait. Who knows

131

what may be happening to Joe? I'd never for-give myself if we didn't at least try to help him."

"Nor I. You're right," said Dr. Grimes. "I have an idea. We can leave a large note here in camp, and blaze our trail as we go so that we can be followed."

"Splendid!" Professor Bullfinch seized the fruit carrier and, extracting the carton from it, ripped a large piece of cardboard free. On it, in bold letters, Dr. Grimes wrote: ONE OF OUR PARTY SEIZED BY NATIVES. FOLLOW BLAZES. BRING WEAPONS.

"That ought to do it," he said.

Meantime, Professor Bullfinch had taken up the obsidian ax, and he hefted it thoughtfully. "I should hate to have to turn this against a per-son," he said. "Still, a scientist should not shrink from new experiences. We can't let anything happen to Joe."

Dr. Grimes got himself a stone-tipped club, and Danny took his spear and the raft knife. Then, somewhat grimly, the three set off into the jungle.

From the banana grove the footprints led up-ward, toward the cone-shaped peak in the is-land's center. This territory was all strange to them. Their first ten days had been spent in such intense activity, working on their various projects and gathering enough food to stay alive, that they had no time for exploration. The jungle grew thicker and they could see clearly the broken twigs and trampled underbrush where the natives had passed with their prisoner.

The ground became steeper and the going more difficult. Outcroppings of rock appeared, black and sharply ribbed, and Danny had to scout on either side to find the traces of the men they were following. Dr. Grimes cut one more blaze in a stunted tree, and then they climbed over a ledge of lava and found themselves looking down the other side of the mountain.

They wiped their streaming faces and stared out over the green sea of treetops. Far below, near the shore, they could see the gleam of a beach and some grayish, rounded humps that must be the roofs of huts.

"Look!" said Danny. "There's a trail here."

They saw a pile of stones, and beyond it another. They went down a little way and saw that there was a regular pathway, very narrow but clearly marked, running down into the forest.

Danny went first, without hesitation, and the two men followed him more slowly. They began to speak in whispers, and to tread more softly, and unconsciously they all gripped their rude weapons more tightly.

The trail wound down the mountainside and soon they passed groves of banana, papaya, guava, and other fruit trees. A little farther on, in a grassy space, some goats bounded away. Then, abruptly, they emerged on the edge of a high bank which led down to a clearing. They stopped short. They were looking directly into the native village.

Rough, simple huts, thatched with banana fronds, were arranged in a large circle around an open space. Other, smaller huts could be seen among the trees beyond. Here and there were small plantings, and a few pigs rooted about the outskirts of the village. But all their attention was fixed on what was happening in the clearing.

A crowd of dark-skinned people were gathered about Joe, who was being held by two men. A short fat man was talking excitedly to the boy, who stood as if dazed, for he made no attempt to struggle. And behind him was a large iron pot resting on flat stones over a pit. In the pit a fire crackled and blazed.

As the three watched, the fat man placed a garland of green leaves on the boy's head.

"Parsley!" gasped Dr. Grimes.

Behind Joe was a large iron pot

They had sunk down in the underbrush to avoid being seen, but now Danny started to his feet.

"Get down!" whispered Professor Bullfinch, clutching at Danny's arm.

"But we've got to save him!" Danny replied, trying to pull his arm free.

"There's nothing we can do," Dr. Grimes said, keeping his voice low. "If we rush down there against that mob, they'll pick our bones clean in no time. Get down!"

Danny stared at Dr. Grimes. Then suddenly his eyes went wide.

"Pick our bones—!" he began. "Of course!"

Without another word, he broke away and went charging down the bank into the clearing.

CHAPTER EIGHTEEN

The Moment of Battle

"He's hysterical," said Dr. Grimes.

Professor Bullfinch had risen to his feet and was preparing to rush after the boy, ax in hand.

Dr. Grimes grabbed him by the shirt and held him back. "Don't be a fool, Bullfinch," he whispered.

"Let go!" The Professor's face was pale but determined, and behind his glasses his eyes gleamed in a warlike way.

"You and I, against fifty savages? Don't be silly. We must make a plan."

Dr. Grimes dragged the Professor back up the trail, out of earshot of the village.

"Well? What sort of plan?" asked the Professor.

"Perhaps we could create a diversion. One of us could throw stones at them, and when they come charging up the bank the other could run around into the clearing and rescue the boys."

"What if they catch the one who throws the

stones? Then only one would be left to rescue three."

"Then suppose we set fire to some of those thatched roofs? In the confusion—"

"In the confusion the boys may be roasted instead of boiled."

"Bullfinch, you're a pest," Dr. Grimes said in exasperation. "If I were alone, I'd have no difficulty deciding on an idea."

"But those ideas are impractical."

"Have you a better one?"

"Yes. It has just occurred to me—"

Before Professor Bullfinch could continue there was a noise behind them, higher up the trail. Branches snapped and stones came rattling down.

"More natives! We're surrounded!" said Dr. Grimes. He raised his club.

"Wait. I don't think so," Professor Bullfinch said, calmly.

At the same instant, a group of men came into sight. They were seamen, and two or three were holding rifles. Their leader, a tall, portly man, whose white hair stuck out under the peak of his cap, was carrying a pistol.

"The men from the ship!" Grimes said.

"Exactly. As I was about to say, it occurred to

me that they'd be along soon," said Professor Bullfinch. He stepped forward and held out his hand. "How do you do?" he said. "I'm Professor Euclid Bullfinch and this is Dr. A. J. Grimes."

"Howdy," said the tall man, shaking hands. "I'm Larkin, first mate of the *Inca Queen*. We know all about you. There was a bulletin from Lima asking everybody to be on the watch for you. Then we picked up your signal, but it failed, and we've been searching the sector for an island. There isn't one marked on the charts in this region."

"Let's not stand about gossiping!" Dr. Grimes put in sharply. "The boys—"

"Oh, yeah. There's supposed to be two kids with you. I got your note. The natives caught 'em, eh?"

"Yes."

"Well, we'll get 'em back," the mate said confidently. "We'll blow those savages to bits. Which way?"

"Follow me," said the Professor, and turned down the trail. The others pressed close behind, holding their rifles ready.

They came to the top of the bank and paused. In the clearing they saw a dreadful sight. The two husky guards were holding Joe face down over the pot. Danny stood nearby with three or four of the natives about him.

"Quick!" Dr. Grimes exclaimed. "There's no time to lose!"

"Get 'em!" shouted Larkin.

He burst through the thicket and started down the bank, holding his pistol high. The rest streamed after him.

The natives turned openmouthed at the intrusion. Larkin leveled his weapon.

"Stand back!" he ordered in a harsh voice. "Don't move or we'll open fire!"

At that Danny leaped forward, holding up both his hands.

"Stop!" he cried. "You don't understand!"

CHAPTER NINETEEN

"A Pot by Any Other Name"

Everyone stared at him. Danny looked round and beckoned to the short, fat man who was staring in fright.

"This is Chief Omata," Danny said. "He speaks English."

The fat man bobbed his head, and with a wide grin said, "That right. I headman these fellas."

"Never mind that stuff," said Larkin. "Let those two boys go."

"No!" Danny interrupted. "It's all right, I tell you."

"Danny, have you lost your mind?" snapped Dr. Grimes.

The Professor, looking worried, said, "I—I think the strain has been too much for him."

"It hasn't!" Danny cried. "Look at me, Professor Bullfinch. Do I look crazy?"

"Well . . ." the Professor began hesitantly.

"Listen," Danny said. "Do you remember what you once told me about a tool having two uses? And about not judging by appearances?"

"But—"

"But listen to me. That pot—that's a tool, too."

"A tool?"

"Sure. It can be a tool to cook with, or—a tool to wash with."

The Professor's mouth opened, but no sound came out.

"That's right," Danny said. "It's a kind of bathtub."

"You mean to say—"

"They're cleaning Joe off," Danny finished.

"Yes, by goodness," Chief Omata put in, beaming. "This boys, friends belong me. I see him friend hurry-up walkabout, face belong him make green, same thing ground. This green belong to big Papa, belong men we plant him. Me fella make wash him along this pot, not make him bulla-makau. Yes?"

Dr. Grimes looked blank. "I know that's English, but what's he saying?"

"It's perfectly clear," Danny said. "He says we are his friends. He says my friend—that's Joe—was running away, and his face was all green, covered with mud. That color of mud belongs to the spirits, to the dead men. He says they wanted to make him clean in the pot, not cook him like meat. See?"

Professor Bullfinch rubbed the top of his head. "I understand. It's a kind of religious ceremony."

"That's right," said Danny. "He told me before that they were afraid Joe would be haunted by dead men if he didn't get that color off. So they are purifying him. They put that wreath on his head to make him smell sweet. It's all part of the ceremony."

"Good heavens!" the Professor sighed. "How could we have been so blind? You have only to look at these people's faces to see that they have no evil intentions. This time I was a careless thinker. I let myself be carried away by appearances." He held out his hand to the plump little chief. "I'm sorry," he said. "I apologize."

"That good fella something," said the chief, shaking the Professor's hand.

"You see," Danny said, "when Dr. Grimes talked about picking us clean, it flashed into my head that that's what they were doing. So I ran down—"

"But suppose you had been wrong?" Dr. Grimes said.

Danny smiled. "If they had been cannibals, they'd have killed Joe before they cooked him. Wouldn't they?"

"Of course," said the Professor. "But we were so excited that it never occurred to us. Worst of all, we had already made up our minds that they were cannibals."

"Yes. Well, as soon as I saw that, then I could see everything," Danny went on. "I saw that they had gentle faces, and that they were all smiling. Remember what you said, Professor, about our surroundings being friendly until they were proved otherwise?"

Professor Bullfinch nodded. "Where did they get an iron pot like that one?" he asked.

"From a ship that stopped here a long time ago. I don't know how long, because they don't seem to have any words for time. A missionary came with that ship and stayed here awhile. He brought bananas and papayas to plant on the island. And he taught the chief English. When you came rushing in, the chief was just saying the Lord's Prayer—"

At these words Omata at once began, in a sing-song voice, as if someone had turned him on like a phonograph: "Papa belong me fella, you stop

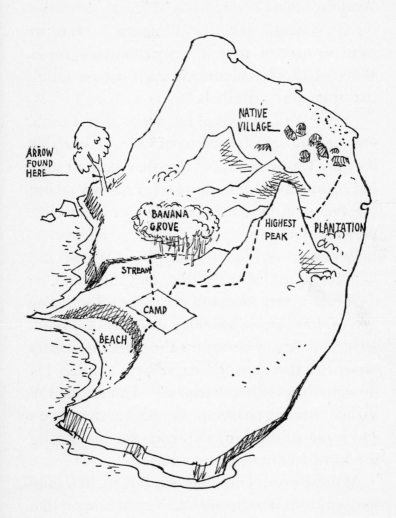

ARROW
FOUND
HERE

NATIVE
VILLAGE

BANANA
GROVE

HIGHEST
PEAK

PLANTATION

STREAM

CAMP

BEACH

along heaven, holy santu him name belong you. . . ."

"Thank you very much," said the Professor politely, stopping him. "But how is it you never came to see us? I mean, if you were friendly, Mr. Omata, why didn't you visit us?"

Omata threw out his hands and opened his eyes wide. He began a long explanation in pidgin English which went on for many minutes. As they got used to the odd phrases, the others began to grasp the sense of what he was saying. Nevertheless, when he was finished the chief turned to Danny, who seemed to understand most easily.

"He says," Danny smiled, "that they were shy and didn't want to disturb us. He thought that Joe and I were the sons of Professor Bullfinch and Dr. Grimes, and when they came quietly to watch us they saw Joe running, and thought spirits were chasing him. So they decided to do our fathers a favor and stop the haunting. To be on the safe side, when they took Joe, they left a plain trail that we could follow."

"And we thought they were savages!" murmured Professor Bullfinch.

"Yes!" the chief said emphatically. "Now me

fellas eat. Good fella bulla-makau, not boys belong you."

He laughed heartily. He turned to the vil-
lagers, and began talking rapidly in his own
tongue. Obviously he was explaining the mistake, because they all began laughing with him,
and some of the men came forward and patted
Danny in a friendly way. The women ran to
fetch large wooden platters and build up the
fires. The sailors put their guns away, and Larkin, holstering his revolver, sent one of them
back along the trail to signal the ship, which was
waiting offshore.

At the same time the guards put Joe back on
his feet. Most of the sticky green mud was gone
from his face and arms. A woman wiped the rest
off with a piece of cloth.

"Whew!" said Joe. "Now I know how a
steamed clam feels."

"Clean enough to eat," Dr. Grimes commented, with an unexpected twinkle in his eye.
"You smell better, too."

"I didn't have any idea what they wanted
when they grabbed me," Joe explained, combing
back his wet hair with his fingers. "They were
all smiling and jabbering at me, and I just froze

147

up. I was so scared, I couldn't even understand what the chief was saying. I couldn't even yell. But when Danny came tearing down and began talking to them, he explained to me what they were after and I—well, I just resigned myself to it."

"I'm not surprised Danny could understand Omata," the Professor said. "After all, he thought of him as a friend. Perhaps there would be less misunderstanding among men if they stopped being so afraid of each other. And if they didn't make up their minds about each other before they found out the facts."

"That's true enough," said Larkin, who was listening. "I once knew a guy with a broken nose. I made up my mind he was a fighter just because his nose was flat. I found out later he was the quietest fellow in the world—he broke his nose playing baseball when he was fourteen years old."

Chief Omata came up to them and beckoned. They followed him to the center of the clearing, where large leaves had been set out for plates. Crude bowls filled with fruit were placed among them, and from the fires came the smells of roasting meat and fish. Women bustled about, preparing food, and three of the men settled themselves before wooden drums and began chanting as they beat a rhythmic accompaniment.

"Dinner music," Larkin said.

Chief Omata held up his hands, and smiled hugely at the visitors. Then he said, "Sit. Eat."

"Well, at any rate," said Dr. Grimes, "I have no trouble understanding that."

And they all took their places for the feast.

CHAPTER TWENTY

The Winner

The freighter *Inca Queen* weighed anchor and stood out from shore. Her whistle blew a long blast of farewell. From the beach brown-skinned men and women waved their hands and lifted up their children to shout good-bye to the visitors. Slowly the island grew smaller until the tiny figures could no longer be seen. It seemed to sink behind the horizon, and at last it was gone.

Only then did the four adventurers leave the rail and go to tell their story to the ship's captain. His name was Edwin Gilbert, and he was a bluff, grizzled, hearty-looking man.

"You're lucky to be alive," he said. "Your plane was expected in Lima and when you were overdue, after the storm, they sent search planes out to look for you. But the ocean's a mighty big place. We'd have found you sooner except that when we first got your signal it died out again before we could get a fix on it. There's no island shown on the maps and we had to keep searching. Then, about a week later, we picked

Slowly the island grew smaller

up the signal again. Anyway, everyone knew you were alive. It was just a matter of finding you."

He turned them over to the chief steward, who stuffed them with a good meal, and then they were examined by the ship's doctor, who pronounced them in excellent shape. They made a tour of the ship with Mr. Larkin, and were fitted out with clean clothing from members of the crew. The boys wore jerseys and dungarees, and Dr. Grimes and the Professor looked like respectable pirates in their nautical clothes.

Later in the day they gathered on deck in a sheltered place aft, just the four of them.

"In a way," said the Professor, "I'm sorry that it's over. I would have liked to spend a little time with Chief Omata's people."

Dr. Grimes was turning over a harpoon head made of bone, given him as a parting gift by the chief. "Astonishing," he said. "They are a Stone Age people, and yet they live a comfortable, if simple, life. It is amazing how men can survive—have survived over the centuries. And only through their ability to make use of their surroundings."

"Oh—speaking of that," said the Professor, "I wonder if our two young friends have kept the tally sticks up to date? Perhaps we can decide who won the duel."

"Sure," said Danny. He ran off to the cabin he shared with Joe, and soon returned carrying the two carved sticks.

"Here we are," he said. "To begin with, we allowed Professor Bullfinch half a notch for thinking of the tally sticks. Then he got one notch for the stone ax, one for the lean-to, one for using the turtle shell as a container, and one for soap."

"Is that all?" asked the Professor.

"Gee, I'm afraid so. Of course you helped on everything else, but so did the rest of us."

"And how about Dr. Grimes?"

"Well, let's see. He thought of the bow-drill, and the trap we set for the natives. And he recognized papayas, which we used for food. Also, he thought of the signal fire, and of smearing the turtle shell with clay so it could be used over the fire. That makes it five to four and a half. But we took half a notch away from him because he got caught in his own trap. So I guess that makes it a draw."

The Professor laughed heartily, but Dr. Grimes scowled. Then he thrust out his hand.

"It was a good fight, Bullfinch," he said.

"Congratulations! We'll try it again next year —but with the proper safeguards—and see who wins then."

"All right. But we'd better try it at home, in my back yard," the Professor smiled. He reached into his pocket and took out a little stick about three inches long. "I've been keeping my own tally," he said. "According to my record, it was Danny who started our first fire because he had the forethought to carry waterproof matches with him. Let me see: then he thought of the pipeline, hot water, spears, the fruit carrier, the bathtub, and the water wheel. And of course, it was he who prevented us from firing on Chief Omata's people and harming them."

"Hmph!" grunted Dr. Grimes. "What about taking a few notches away from *him?* He got us into some tight spots by acting without thinking. Running off and leaving the radio to burn—"

"No," said Professor Bullfinch, "I don't agree. After all, it was terribly important for us to know whether there were other people on the island."

"But Dr. Grimes is right," Danny put in in a soft voice. "Hiding the crank—that was silly and stupid. I ought to have all those notches sliced off for that."

"As long as you realize it, Danny," said the

Professor in a kindly tone, "that's all that matters. However, to be fair, let's take one notch away.

"Now Joe. He didn't do badly either. He thought of gathering birds' eggs, showed us how to catch and clean fish, made a stone hoe for cleaning out logs, and—er—I suppose you could say he finally found the natives.

"By my reckoning," finished the Professor, "Danny is the winner!"

"Great!" shouted Joe.

Dr. Grimes agreed. "In spite of his shortcomings, I think Dan is the most practical of us all. In some ways, that is."

Danny blushed until his face was the same color as his hair. He was saved from further embarrassment by the appearance of Mr. Larkin in the companionway behind them.

"Hey, boys," called the mate, "how'd you like to talk to your folks?"

"What? How?" they both asked.

"We've arranged a radiotelephone relay. Hurry up, before the operator gets tired of waiting."

They followed him to the radio shack. The radio operator glanced up and said, "Which one is Joseph Pearson?"

"I am."

"Okay. Here's your mother."

"Joe?" Mrs. Pearson's high voice came from the speaker. "Can you hear me?"

"Hello, Mom. Sure."

"You sound hoarse. Have you got a cold?"

"No, Mom. I'm fine."

"We've been so worried. I had all I could do to keep your father from rushing down to find you."

"But we weren't lost, Ma. Just a little off our course."

"Oh," said Mrs. Pearson. "Well, are you all right? Did you get enough to eat?"

"Oh, sure, Ma. We had oysters, turtle steak, fresh fruit, fish—"

"Fish? But you don't like fish!"

"Gee, that's right," said Joe. "I forgot."

"Well, don't worry, dear. We're filling the freezer with steaks. Is there anything special you'd like?"

Joe thought for a moment. Then he said, "Yes. Get some of that breakfast cereal with the Geiger counter offer on the box top."

"All right. Take care of yourself, darling. Mrs. Dunn wants to talk to Danny now, so I'll say good-bye.   Your father sends his love.   Good-bye."

"Good-bye, Ma," said Joe.   He turned away from the set, and blew his nose loudly.

They heard Mrs. Dunn say, "Danny?   Hello, Danny."

The familiar voice made Danny's throat close up, and tears start to his eyes.   "H-h-hello, Mom," he said.

"Oh, darling, I'm so glad you're safe."

"So'm I, Mom.   How are you?"

"Now that you're safe, I'm fine, too.   We've been so worried—but never mind that now.   How is the Professor?   And Dr. Grimes?"

"They're swell."

"The lab looks so empty without you and the Professor.   And it's so quiet I don't know where I am half the time.   Well, that won't last long, I'm sure.   You should be home in four or five days, I guess."

"Er . . . Mom," said Danny hesitantly, "I was just thinking—"

"Yes, dear?   What is it?"

"Well, of course you know I miss you, Mom. And home, and everything.   But Captain Gilbert said that after they drop us the ship is going on to Lima. And I've never seen Peru, and after all we have almost a month of vacation left, and there's nothing to do at home except play croquet—"

He trailed off into silence. After a moment his mother said, "Daniel Dunn!"

"Aw, gee, Mom—" Danny began.

"Not another word! Put the Professor on the phone."

Professor Bullfinch had been chuckling in the background. He stepped forward and said into the microphone, "Hello, Mrs. Dunn. How are you?"

"I'm fine. Did you hear that boy?"

"Yes," said the Professor. "But don't worry. I'll get him home safely. It's impossible—or rather I should say, to be scientifically accurate, it's highly improbable—that anything else will happen to us on this trip."

There was a silence. Then Mrs. Dunn began laughing.

"Professor Bullfinch," she said, "Danny is my son, and I love him very much. But when that boy is around, the improbable happens almost immediately and the impossible takes just a little bit longer. Keep an eye on him."

"I will, Mrs. Dunn," the Professor laughed. "Good-bye."

He put his arm around Danny's shoulder and steered him to the door, and together they went up on deck to rejoin their friends.

About the Authors

JAY WILLIAMS, co-author of *Danny Dunn and the Anti-Gravity Paint* and *Danny Dunn on a Desert Island,* is also the author of six other junior books and of six adult books. Born in Buffalo, New York, Mr. Williams was educated at the University of Pennsylvania, Columbia University, and the Art Students League. Several years in show business as an entertainer and stage manager were followed by four years as assistant press agent for the Group Theatre and then service with the 65th Infantry Division. He and his wife now live in Redding, Connecticut, with their son Christopher and daughter Victoria.

RAYMOND ABRASHKIN is the author and co-producer of the very popular and successful film *Little Fugitive.* He has done a Picture News Series called "Life with Junior" with a group of experts including Dr. Benjamin Spock, and also, for *The Ladies' Home Journal,* a series called "Bringing Up Parents" with Dr. Barbara Biber of the Bank Street College, New York City. In addition to over fifty children's records, he has written the librettos for four children's operas. Born in Brooklyn in 1911, Mr. Abrashkin received his B.S. degree from City College of New York and taught in the New York public schools. Following service in the U.S. Maritime Service, he was an editor at Reynal and Hitchcock and since 1946 has devoted his full time to free-lance work. He and his wife now live with their two sons, John and Hank, in Weston, Connecticut.